S9F-

She looked wild, sultry and sexy...

Excitement thrilled through her and, with a sweeping gesture, Briony flung back the curtain. Gliding her bare feet across the plush carpet, swaying her slender body sinuously, she moved out into the showroom like some jungle animal.

'Oh, dear God.

She blinked and with her arms sti And his face was like th

Dear Reader

Autumn's here and the nights are drawing in—but when better to settle down with your favourite romances? This month, Mills & Boon have made sure that you won't notice the colder weather—our wide range of love stories are sure to warm the chilliest of hearts! Whether you're wanting a rattling good read, something sweet and magical, or to be carried off to hot, sunny countries—like Australia, Greece or Venezuela—we've got the books to please you.

Enjoy!

The Editor

Grace Green was born in Scotland and is a former teacher. In 1967 she and her marine engineer husband John emigrated to Canada where they raised their four children. Empty-nesters now, they are happily settled in West Vancouver in a house overlooking the ocean. Grace enjoys walking the sea wall, gardening, getting together with other writers...and watching her characters come to life, because she knows that, once they do, they will take over and write her stories for her.

A WOMAN'S LOVE

BY

GRACE GREEN

MILLS & BOON LIMITED
ETON HOUSE   18-24 PARADISE ROAD
RICHMOND   SURREY   TW9 1SR

To my daughter Kathleen

All the characters in this book have no existence outside the imagination of the Author, and have no relation whatsoever to anyone bearing the same name or names. They are not even distantly inspired by any individual known or unknown to the Author, and all the incidents are pure invention.

All Rights Reserved. The text of this publication or any part thereof may not be reproduced or transmitted in any form or by any means, electronic or mechanical, including photocopying, recording, storage in an information retrieval system, or otherwise, without the written permission of the publisher.

This book is sold subject to the condition that it shall not, by way of trade or otherwise, be lent, resold, hired out or otherwise circulated without the prior consent of the publisher in any form of binding or cover other than that in which it is published and without a similar condition including this condition being imposed on the subsequent purchaser.

*First published in Great Britain 1992
by Mills & Boon Limited*

© Grace Green 1992

*Australian copyright 1992
Philippine copyright 1992
This edition 1992*

ISBN 0 263 77799 5

*Set in Times Roman 10 on 10½ pt.
01-9211-61029 C*

Made and printed in Great Britain

CHAPTER ONE

BRIONY hesitated as she reached the white picket gate, tempted—for one brief, cowardly moment—to turn tail.

Her long blonde hair glistened in the evening sun as she glanced over her shoulder at the Lollipop, the red Volkswagen Jake had given her five years before on her seventeenth birthday. It was sitting at the kerb, still panting in the summer heat after its arduous climb up Marwyck Hill. How easy it would be, she thought wryly, to jump back in and zoom away again. To return to the residence, and start packing——

Suddenly impatient with herself, she curled her fingers around the gate's metal latch. There was only one way to find out why the professor had invited her to his home and it wasn't by skulking out here like a would-be burglar! With a purposeful squaring of her shoulders, she pushed the gate open and began walking up the path to the house.

It was one of a group on the outskirts of the Marwyck Art College grounds, an attractive, rambling building in warm red brick. She'd never been inside, but she'd jogged past it often, usually late in the evening when she'd finished studying and felt like a breath of fresh air before going to bed. Once, at dusk, she'd caught sight of a plump, pleasant-looking woman—his wife?—working at a sewing machine by an upstairs window.

The front door opened just as she reached it, and her host greeted her with a smile. With his straggly grey hair, rumpled suede jacket and baggy cords he looked, Briony decided, every bit the stereotypical art professor. She returned his smile, hoping hers would hide her apprehension. 'Good evening, Professor Sharp.'

'You're punctual.' He stood back to usher her inside. 'Just as you've always been in class.'

Showing her into a small study that smelled of stale tobacco, he sat her down in an armchair and poured two glasses of sherry.

'I can see you're a bundle of nerves!' His moss-green eyes encompassed her as he took a seat at the opposite side of the hearth from where she was perched on the edge of her chair. 'You are, of course, wondering why I asked you to call round. Tell me, have you come up with an answer?'

Briony sipped from her glass before speaking. 'The finals are over, so you can't want to give me advice about what I should be studying. And though I'm not *over*-confident, I'm pretty sure I did well.' She tried to give a casual little laugh, but it sounded strained. 'There's nothing wrong, is there? Did I make some ghastly mistake? Am I going to fail? Is——?'

'Good God, no.' The professor lifted a packet of cigarettes from a table at his elbow and tapped it absently on his knee. 'I can tell you—off the record—that you'll come through with flying colours.' He opened the pack and held it out to her. When she shook her head with a murmured, 'No, thank you,' he extricated a cigarette and placed it between his lips. Unhurriedly he lit it, tossing the spent match into a brass ashtray before going on, 'So, tell me, have you made any plans for the summer?'

Small talk, Briony thought tautly. Why doesn't he get right to the point? 'I'm going home—to Devil's Crag, in Cornwall. There aren't many jobs on the market at present, so I've decided to take a break for the next few weeks. I'll probably spend the summer roaming the moors...thinking, making plans for the future. And, of course, painting.'

'How would you like to go abroad in August—explore the museums of Paris, Florence, Venice...see the masterpieces I've been lecturing on this past year? A grand art appreciation tour, with me as your mentor?'

For a moment, Briony sat motionless, hardly believing what she'd just heard. To go on an art tour with this man, who was known the length and breadth of the country for his painting and for his teaching...

'But weren't you and your wife planning to take Angelique St Clair?' The words were out before she could stop them. Angelique, a lovely but painfully shy redhead, was a talented student who, during this final year, had been the professor's special protégée. Though she, too, came from Cornwall—her home was in Falmouth—she and Briony moved in different circles, and Briony didn't know too much about the other student's background, but a few weeks ago she had overheard Angelique talking to a friend about her forthcoming trip.

'When it came to the crunch, Angelique had a...problem coming up with her expenses.' The professor's eyes glittered with an unfamiliar expression that for some reason made Briony uncomfortable. Shifting awkwardly, she gulped down a mouthful of her drink, but as she reached over to place her glass on the table she knocked her elbow on the arm of her chair, and some of the sherry spilled on the carpet, the rest jolting from the glass to spatter on to the front of her white cotton sweater.

'Oh——' she jumped up, cursing herself silently for her carelessness '—I'm sorry...'

Her host got to his feet too. 'No problem. Here——' Stubbing out his cigarette in the ashtray, he crossed the space between them. 'Let me help...'

Before Briony realised what his intention was, he'd captured one of her shoulders in a firm grip and with his handkerchief had begun to dab the stains from the white top. She was barely aware of the mingled smell of nicotine and sherry on his breath; all she could think of was his closeness, and the intimacy of his actions. She felt her mouth go dry, forced herself not to shrink from him as he rubbed the handkerchief lightly across the fine fabric, over the swell of her breasts.

'There,' he said finally. He gave the sweater one last flick, and as he did his fingertips brushed her nipple. Briony froze, horror rippling through her. *Had he made a pass at her*? But as she jerked her head up, her grey eyes wide, she saw nothing in his expression except concern, and she swallowed hard. What a suspicious mind she had!

He moved away to refill her glass, and when he turned back again the look in his eyes was so bland that Briony felt ashamed that she'd thought his touch could have been anything but accidental. Quickly, she banished the little incident from her mind, and directed her attention to what he was saying.

'...Angelique. I've been very disappointed in her work lately.' He walked across the room and gave Briony her glass. 'I can tell you—in the strictest confidence—it was quite a relief to me when she backed out.

'So...' Resuming his seat, he leaned back lazily and quirked a questioning brow in her direction. 'Does the idea of an art tour appeal?'

'Oh, yes!' she exclaimed. 'Oh, yes, it *does* appeal!'

'Then will *you* be able to afford the trip? It'll be fairly expensive, because when Celine—my wife—and I travel we go first class all the way. We'll start off by flying to Paris, and after a week we'll go on to Florence, and...'

As she listened, Briony felt as if her very blood were singing. Of course the idea appealed; she could think of nothing in the world she'd rather do, and—thank heavens!—she had the money. Or at least the money was there in trust for her, to be used for her education, or however Jake saw fit. And of course he'd approve of this tour of Europe. How could he not?

She couldn't *wait* to tell him about the invitation.

Placing her glass on the hearth, she sat forward eagerly, her hands clasped over her knees. And excitement—a sweet, almost unbearable excitement—

flowed through her veins and into her heart as she listened to Professor Sharp outline his plans.

Plans for the trip of a lifetime.

'No, Briony, you can't have the money. And that's final!'

Briony stared up incredulously at the lean, implacable features of the man looking down at her. A moment ago she'd been swinging along the Cornish moor beside him, her grey eyes alight with anticipation as she confidently awaited his decision. Now...

'But I *have* to have it!' she exploded. 'I *told* you why I need it! And this morning you promised——'

'This morning I promised I would think it over... and I have.' Jacob Trelawney's hard sapphire gaze reflected the relentless glare of the sun beating down on them from the cloudless July sky. 'The answer is no.'

'But——'

'I've made my decision.' The almost imperceptible twitch of a muscle at the base of his throat was the only sign that Briony's protest had affected him in any way. 'And now——' he glanced pointedly at his Rolex watch '—it's time for us to be getting home.'

He swung away arrogantly, his long legs taking him with self-assured strides towards the turreted granite house glittering on a rocky peak above the ocean, about a mile and a half away.

For a stunned moment, Briony stared after him, utterly unmoved by the attractive play of light on his black, crisply cut hair, and by the way his white cotton shirt rippled over the muscles of his wide, powerful shoulders. All she could see as she watched him stride from her was the death of her dreams.

She clenched her hands into tight fists, resentment surging through her in great, fierce waves. He couldn't do this to her. He couldn't deny her this chance of a lifetime. Was he *blind*, that he didn't see what an opportunity she'd been offered?

She hurried after him, the heather springing under her quick, angry steps. 'Don't walk away from me when we're talking, Jake!'

She couldn't believe it—he was ignoring her, striding right on across the moor as if he hadn't heard her! She broke into a run, her heart thumping erratically under her blue knit top, and adrenalin pumping through every inch of her slender body. Her toe tangled in a twisted root just as she reached him, and, losing her balance, she lurched forward and grasped at the first thing her fingers came in contact with: his rolled-up shirtsleeve. She held on and tugged it hard as she stumbled upright again, and he wheeled round, his brows gathered in an impatient frown.

'It's *my money*, Jake!' she gasped. 'Why won't you let me have it?' The salt-tanged wind sweeping in from the ocean whipped the words from her mouth. 'Why are you treating me like a...' she fought to regain her breath '...like an idiot who isn't capable of making her own decisions?'

Jake jerked his shirt from her grasp. 'Because you're not old enough—or experienced enough—to make the right ones,' he snapped. 'I'm not denying it's your money. Of course it is. But your mother left me to judge how it should be spent... at least till you're twenty-five, and that's not for another three years.'

She had never questioned Jake's decisions before. In the ten years since her mother died, leaving him as her guardian, Briony had looked up to him, respected him, never defied him. But she was an adult now, and since her twenty-first birthday she had no longer been his ward. The fact that he still had control of the purse-strings had never bothered her before today. But now she wanted... no, she *needed*, to make her own decisions.

'Don't you see, Jake?' she cried, frustratedly sweeping back the thick blonde hair dancing around her face in the wind. 'I don't care if I make mistakes. *Everyone does*. It's called experience. But at least they'll be *my* mistakes, and, if I have to, I'll answer for them. Oh, you're fourteen years older than I am, and I know you're a lot wiser——'

'At least you grant me that much.' The clipped tones were sardonic. 'And I grant you that, yes, there are times when you must be allowed to make mistakes. But there are some mistakes you can make when you're very young that may have a drastic effect on your whole life.' His voice softened as he went on, 'These are the mistakes from which your parents—or those who care for you in their place—must protect you——'

'Words, Jake.' Briony's voice was low but intense as she interrupted him. 'They don't mean anything to me right now. *Feelings*—that's what I'm talking about.' She thrust her hands out, palms down, revealing her tapering, fine-boned fingers. 'Look at these, the hands of an artist—a *talented* artist.' She felt herself blush. Her innate modesty normally kept her from blowing her own trumpet...but if, by blowing it, she could persuade Jake to change his mind, then blow it she would! 'Professor Sharp thinks I show great promise, Jake; he says he's never had a student before who brought such depth and such emotion to her work...'

She paused for a moment, expecting Jake to put an abrupt end to her words, but he was standing like a statue, hands jammed into the pocket of his black trousers, an expression on his face that was completely unreadable. She ran her tongue over her upper lip before going on, 'This trip to the Continent is something I've dreamed about ever since I started studying art. I dreamed of one day going on my own...but to go with Professor Sharp and his wife, to have him as my guide and mentor——'

'The professor will have to go without you.' Jake was facing the sun, and the rays cast a golden glow on his lean, tanned features. 'If your mother were here, she'd——'

'If Ma were here, she'd have seen this trip as the educational opportunity of a lifetime,' Briony interrupted heatedly. 'But if she *hadn't* wanted me to go, I know she'd have given me a reason.' She tilted her small chin in a defiant gesture. 'What's yours?'

For the first time she saw Jake's blue eyes become shadowed, saw a suspicion of hesitation there, and she felt a surge of triumph. Triumph salted with uneasiness. *Did* he have a valid reason?

She waited, nerves on edge. She had just seen a chink in his armour; was she going to see it widen?

When he finally spoke, his voice had a weary undertone. 'I don't intend to give you my reasons; you're just going to have to accept my decision.' As he spoke, Briony noticed that the grooves bracketing his mouth seemed deeper than they had when she had arrived home earlier that day... before she had brought up the subject of her proposed trip.

'Let's put it behind us,' he went on in the gentle tone he'd have used to deal with a recalcitrant four-year-old. 'Polly's preparing a special homecoming dinner for you, and you know how upset she becomes if we're late——'

'I'll find the money, Jake.' Briony's words were so quietly uttered, his reaction so delayed, that she thought at first he hadn't heard. Then she saw white lines of tension appear around his nostrils.

'For God's sake, Briony, can't you leave it?'

'There's more than one way to skin a cat.' Briony felt another little surge of triumph. But this time there was no uneasiness accompanying it. She didn't have to depend on him; she'd go on the trip, but she'd do it without his help. 'I know it's a large sum,' she said steadily, 'but I'll find some way to come up with the money. I told Professor Sharp I'd have no problem paying my expenses——'

She broke off, clearing her throat. She didn't want to admit to Jake that she had told the professor to go ahead and make all the bookings for her—didn't want to confess that she'd promised to give him a cheque for the full amount on the first of August, when they met at the airport.

The first of August... That was just four weeks away! Briony's heartbeats performed an erratic tango and with an effort she quelled the panic that had caused it. She'd get the money...somehow. There had to be a way. There just had to be! 'When the professor and his wife fly from Heathrow to Paris at the beginning of August——' she managed to inject a proud confidence into her words '—I shall be with them.'

'Briony...'

Surely that wasn't a pleading tone in Jake's voice? Briony felt a faint glimmer of hope. Was he beginning to thaw? She stared sharply at him, but his blue eyes were steel-hard, his mouth set in an uncompromising line. She sighed. She had been mistaken; Jacob Trelawney had never pleaded for anything in his life and he wasn't about to start now.

She twisted her shoulders in a dismissive shrug. 'I'm sorry, Jake—if you won't cut the apron strings, I'll have to do it myself. Now, I agree with you, we should put the subject behind us. I don't want to talk about it again.'

Tossing her hair back from her face in a determined gesture, she strode fiercely away from him. Ahead of her a startled grouse rose from the heather, and skimmed away low across the moor. On any other occasion she would have stopped to watch it, memorising each beautiful line so that she could later translate it to paper, using delicate strokes of her pen to capture the texture and each fine detail of the beautiful creature...but today she was barely aware of it. All she wanted to do was put as much distance between Jake and herself as possible.

In fact, she decided bitterly, she'd be happy if she never set eyes on him again!

* * *

Fifteen minutes later she reached the drive leading to the house, and as she slowed her pace she heard a muffled sound reverberating in the air. Rounding a clump of overgrown blue hydrangeas, she saw Polly standing at the front door. Jake's aunt was wielding an antique silver dinner gong in her hand, and she was beating it for all she was worth, her head bobbing up and down with each vigorous movement. Briony felt her resentment at Jake spill over again. Wasn't it fortunate, she reflected tautly, that she hadn't told Polly yet about the proposed trip, having wanted to hug the delicious secret to herself till everything was settled? Now at least she wouldn't have to distress the other woman by telling her of Jake's arrogant, unfeeling refusal.

With an effort, she tried to focus her mind away from her disappointment. She loved Jake's aunt deeply, and she knew how upset the elderly lady would be if she sensed that the two people who meant more to her than anything on earth had been quarrelling.

'Coming, Polly,' she shouted, flinging her arm up in cheerful greeting. Then, forcing her lips into a smile, she crossed the forecourt, her trainers crunching on the white gravel chips. 'Sorry if we're a little late,' she said breathlessly.

'You have exactly fifteen minutes to go upstairs and change for dinner... and do something with that hair, dear!' The flared skirt of Polly's orange dress swirled around her petite figure as she spun away from Briony and back through the front door, her high heels clicking busily on the slate floor of the large entrance hall. 'And don't forget to wash your face,' she called over her shoulder. 'You have a streak of green paint on your nose.'

Automatically, Briony lifted her hand to her face... and then dropped it again with an exasperated exclamation.

Jake's aunt had come to take over the housekeeping duties at the Crag after Briony's mother had died; Polly had never been married, had never had a child, and she'd jumped at the chance of mothering a little girl.

But she *still* treated her as if she were a little girl! Just as Jake did.

'Jake...'

Even as she muttered his name balefully she heard his heavy tread on the gravel outside.

Quickly, she crossed the hall and ran up the winding oak staircase. The last thing she wanted to do was talk with him in the mood she was in.

Once upstairs, she walked quickly along the landing and into her bedroom, just barely resisting the urge to bang the door behind her. She had never felt more like screaming. She was not a child but an adult... and had been for some time! Why was it that neither Polly nor Jake had noticed that she had made the transition? Why was it that when they looked at her they still seemed to see little Briony, orphaned at twelve? Why could neither of them see that she was no longer that sheltered, coltish child?

Why couldn't they see that she had become a woman?

Hair still damp from her shower, Briony hurried along the hallway from the bathroom, her blue robe tied snugly around her slender waist. Once in her bedroom, she closed the door and threw off the robe. Then, dressed only in her lacy silk bra and matching bikini panties, she crossed to the bed, where her as yet unpacked case was lying open.

Extricating a pair of clean jeans, she pulled them on, and tugged up the zip. Then, frowning, she rummaged for a top among the garments she'd packed so haphazardly before leaving the residence, but even as she reached for her best white cotton sweater she remembered the sherry stains.

Stains she'd meant to wash out when she got back to her room after being at the professor's house, but she'd been so excited about the prospect of going on the art tour that she hadn't given the garment a second thought.

She clutched the sweater in her hands, staring into space. The art tour...

She blew out a frustrated sigh as she recalled Jake's closed expression when she'd told him about the invitation. He was normally such a *reasonable* man. Why on earth couldn't he see what an opportunity the prof was giving her?

The question buzzed around in her mind like a persistent mosquito as she tossed the white sweater aside, and grimly—as if it really *were* a persistent mosquito!—she swatted the question away. Tonight, she wouldn't think about it.

Tomorrow, she would decide what to do...decide just how she was going to come up with the money she needed so desperately.

Slipping on a cherry-pink blouse, she fastened a silver chain around her neck, and then applied a hint of ash-blue eyeshadow, and a touch of cherry pink lip-gloss. She didn't need any blusher, she decided, as her cheeks were still sun-flushed from her walk on the moors that afternoon. After blow-drying her hair, she brushed it back from her face, letting it fall naturally so that it swung at her shoulders.

And, as an afterthought, she sprayed a little Chanel behind her ears.

The grandfather clock in the curve of the stairwell chimed seven as she crossed the landing. Perfect timing, she reflected...but, instead of feeling a surge of anticipation at the thought of the special dinner ahead, all she felt was a vague sense of dread.

This afternoon had marked the end of her old relationship with Jake. A relationship which had, for her, been a quiet but joyous one. That relationship was now soured. No matter what happened in the future, things would never again be the same between them.

But despite her conviction that it was all his fault, and despite her intense resentment towards him, she knew she'd lost something precious.

And the knowledge made her feel as if an icy wind were blowing through her heart.

CHAPTER TWO

'SURPRISE!'

Briony stopped abruptly in the doorway of the drawing-room as several voices shouted out and the light went on. For a moment she couldn't make sense of what was happening. When she'd crossed the hallway, the door had been open and the room had been in darkness. She had wondered absently why the heavy velvet curtains were closed when it was still light outside, but had suspected nothing.

So, she thought as she saw the small group of people waiting for her, it was going to be a party. She felt a slackening of her tension. She hadn't been looking forward to sitting over a meal with just Jake and his aunt—Polly, absent-minded though she was, could sometimes be remarkably astute. With the other three present—Charles Denham, owner of Denham's Folly, the estate bordering Devil's Crag, his wife Prue and their thirty-four-year-old daughter Diane—things should go much more smoothly. She knew Jake would be just as anxious as she to hide the fact that they'd quarrelled.

He was standing by the drinks cabinet and as she forced herself to include him in her smile of greeting she noticed that he was wearing a taupe lightweight suit which she'd never seen before, and which accentuated his tan. Reluctantly, she also noticed that his blue silk tie intensified the deep sapphire-blue of his eyes ... eyes which were unblinkingly following her progress across the room. She jerked her attention away from him, and crossed to his aunt.

'Polly——' she gave the elderly woman a warm hug '—how lovely! I've never had a surprise party before.'

'You haven't?' Charles fingered the gold watch looped across his waistcoat. 'Well, we'd better see that this one's a humdinger, eh, Jake, what do you say?'

Briony didn't hear Jake's response as Prue enveloped her in an affectionate embrace. The older woman was as plump as Polly was thin, and Briony felt as if she were disappearing into a mound of feather pillows.

'Congratulations on getting such wonderful marks, Briony,' Prue said in her broad Cornish accent. 'Your Ma would have been proud of you.'

'Briony,' Diane approached, 'add my congrats to Mummy's. We're all frightfully pleased for you.'

'Thanks so much.' Briony felt her nostrils twitch as she accepted Diane's fleeting kiss on the cheek. Diane Denham was a statuesque brunette with eyes the colour of bitter chocolate, perfect cheekbones and a glossy Cleopatra hairstyle... and a great passion for horses. And, though Briony had no doubt that the other woman had showered before changing into her Grecian-style white silk dress, there still lingered around her a very faint horsy smell.

'This is for you, m'dear.' Charles brought forward a sleek package with the name of Falmouth's exclusive Jasmine Boutique emblazoned on it. 'We hope you'll enjoy it.'

'Polly told us last week when we lunched together that she wasn't going to allow you to wear jeans at the dinner table any more now that you're no longer a student——'

Diane interrupted her mother gaily. 'So when I was in town yesterday I bought you something special.'

'Isn't it exciting?' said Polly. 'Do hurry and open it, dear!'

What could it be? Briony felt anticipation bubble up inside her. Her own modest monthly allowance from the trust fund would never permit her to shop at the Jasmine Boutique... and, though Diane might sometimes smell like a horse, she had excellent taste. Whatever it was, it would be fashionable, beautiful... In her excitement, she couldn't seem to get the package opened——

'Allow me, Briony.'

It was the first time Jake had spoken to her since their confrontation on the moors, and Briony noticed that his voice held not even the slightest hint of hostility towards her. It was indulgent, and absently teasing, as it had always been in the past.

He didn't look at her as he took the package, his attention focused on undoing the tangled strings securing it. Nice hands, Briony thought, he has nice hands. Lean, strong, competent. Strange, she mused, that she'd never really noticed them before—yet she must have looked at them a thousand times! She must have looked at them when he taught her how to steer *Trelawney's Woman*, his yacht; she must have looked at them when he showed her how to build a camp fire after hiking all day on the moors; she must have looked at them when he taught her to drive the Lollipop during the weeks following her seventeenth birthday, before she left for Marwyck...

As golden memories spilled into her mind, Briony hugged her arms round herself. Jake had been so good to her, for as long as she could remember... ever since she'd been seven years old, in fact, when her widowed mother had married Jacob Trelawney senior and he had brought them to Devil's Crag. The magnificent granite house had been in the family for centuries, and when, five years after their marriage, Jake's father and Briony's mother died within months of each other, Jake had inherited the property... and Briony along with it! He had become her guardian, she his ward. He had continued treating her with the same sort of absent, teasing affection he always had... with an added protectiveness, as if she were a stray kitten which he had somehow, unwittingly, found in his care. But, despite his apparent casualness, she'd known she could always count on him, and she had always believed in her heart that they shared a very special rapport.

Until this afternoon. This afternoon everything had changed. She had seen a different Jake. A Jake she didn't know. A Jake who had turned into a dictator——

The rustle of tissue paper snapped her mind back to the present, and as she blinked she saw that Jake had opened the package and was holding it out to her. 'There you are, Bri.'

'Thanks,' she murmured.

Their fingers brushed together as she took it, and she felt an odd, disturbing tingle run up her arm. Startled, she raised her eyes abruptly... but Jake wasn't even looking at her; he had turned to Diane, who had come to stand at his side and had looped her arm through his.

'Do hurry, Briony!' she urged impatiently. 'When I saw it I knew it was just right for you. As soon as Ellie Jasmine brought it through from the back it positively screamed "Briony Campbell" at me.' Her throaty laugh was infectious and Briony heard the others chuckle.

She laid the package on the coffee-table, and drew back the tissue paper. It was a dress. Silk, like the one Diane herself was wearing; not white, though, but periwinkle-blue, one of her favourite colours. Briony felt her heartbeats quicken. Would it be the same style as Diane's, cut so that the sensuous fabric revealed each feminine curve in a way that was elegant yet subtly provocative?

She lifted it up carefully, but as the folds shimmered out in a silken cloud she stared, for a moment disbelieving, and then, as disappointment welled up inside her, she felt her heart plunge.

'Thank you so much, Diane—it's beautiful,' she somehow managed. 'Absolutely beautiful. Quite perfect.'

Quite perfect for a young teenager, an inner voice taunted her; you would have looked lovely in that style when you were fourteen, with the Peter Pan collar, gathered skirt, short, puffy sleeves.

'There, didn't I tell you the child would love it?' Polly crowed. 'Prue and Diane showed it me yesterday, dear——' Polly turned to Briony '—and gave me the receipt so you could change it if it didn't fit, but I'm sure it will—it looks just your size. Now will you all excuse me while I go check the roast?'

As Polly tripped out of the room, the Denhams wandered back to the hearth. Jake opened the heavy velvet curtains to let the evening sunshine pour in, and Diane moved to join him, and started chattering about Mercury, her recently acquired black stallion.

Folding the dress and putting it back in the box, Briony found herself almost overcome by a dreadful, aching loneliness. They all still thought of her as a child—Jake, and Polly, and the Denhams. She was sure they didn't mean to be condescending, but they were; they made her feel as if she were still a schoolgirl.

With a frustrated sigh, she glanced round, to find that though Diane was still chattering to Jake he was no longer looking at the vivacious brunette. He was, in fact, staring directly at herself, and as Briony's startled grey eyes met the dark, searching intensity of his gaze she felt her throat muscles constrict. She was glad her skin was flushed by the sun... perhaps her quick, embarrassed blush would go unnoticed.

She wanted to look away but couldn't. It was he, finally, who broke the contact. Frowning, he dragged a hand through his thick black hair, and, giving his head a little shake, as though attempting to clear it, he returned his attention to Diane, adjusting his stance slightly so that his back was to Briony.

Shivering as if someone had just walked over her grave, Briony placed the Jasmine Boutique package on a table by the door, and moved across the room to join Charles and Prue.

Why on earth had Jake been looking at her like that?

But no matter how she tried—and she tried all evening!—she couldn't come up with an answer to the puzzling question.

* * *

'It was a lovely party.' Prue poked her head out of the open window of the family Rover as Charles revved up the engine. 'And wonderful to see you all again. Where *are* you, Diane?'

'Coming, Mummy.'

It was way past midnight, and the sky was a deep cobalt-blue with the palest sliver of a new moon and the lightest scattering of stars. Briony could see Diane's shadowy figure close to Jake's, on the other side of the car from where she herself stood with Polly, and she thought she saw them kiss. Then she heard Diane murmur, 'What time shall I come over?'

'Around eight.' Jake's voice was carried to Briony on the breeze. 'We'll sail round to Smuggler's Cove, have lunch at Petro's, and be home by mid-afternoon.'

'Lovely.' Diane glided away from him, and her tall, striking figure became clearly outlined in the light coming from inside the vehicle. Opening the rear door, she paused and called across the car roof, 'Jake and I are going sailing tomorrow, Briony. Do you want to come?'

Briony shook her head. 'No, thanks, Diane. Maybe next time.'

'Right-o,' Diane called out cheerfully, before slipping into the car.

Though Briony couldn't see Jake's face, she sensed him looking at her, and she could imagine the surprise he'd be feeling. It was the first time she'd ever turned down such an invitation. She adored sailing, but for the next few weeks it would have to take a back seat. She had other things to do.

As the Rover moved away down the drive, Polly yawned. 'My goodness, they stayed late. If Charles had told one more golfing story, I think I would have dropped right off to sleep. Thank goodness I did the dishes earlier—the thought of facing them now...' She shuddered.

'Would you care for a nightcap, Poll?' Jake walked up the shallow front steps ahead of them, and held the studded oak door open. 'A Tia Maria, maybe?'

'Oh, no, it's way past my bedtime! Briony, dear,' she added as Jake locked the door behind them, 'I forgot to unplug the coffee-maker. Would you mind...?'

'Of course not—I'll do it right now. Goodnight, Polly, and thanks again for such a wonderful surprise party.' Then, in a tone that was curt enough to let Jake know she was still furious with him for his refusal to let her have her money—but not so curt that Polly would notice!—she threw him a quick, 'Goodnight.'

Without giving him the chance to offer her a nightcap—in her present frame of mind the last thing she wanted to do was sit with him!—she turned and hurried away, her steps echoing in the stillness, and, pushing open the swing door at the end of the long corridor, she entered the kitchen.

This was Polly's domain, a large square room looking out over the ocean. Jake had had it renovated two years ago, but though it now boasted the very latest appliances the colour scheme had stayed the same—blue and white, to complement Polly's prized collection of willow-pattern porcelain. Tonight the fragrance of roast beef and Yorkshire pudding still lingered in the air, mingled with the aroma of the coffee in the electric coffee-maker.

Briony was about to empty out the contents of the carafe when she changed her mind and poured herself a mug of the still piping-hot brew instead. It would keep her awake, she was sure... but she was just as certain that even without it there was no chance she'd sleep. Not with the events of the day still churning relentlessly around in her mind!

Balancing the mug in one hand, she unlocked the back door leading off the kitchen, and, slipping outside to the brick patio, let the door click shut behind her. As she made her way among the shadows to the cushioned wrought-iron furniture, she could see white moths fluttering around the night-scented stock, could smell the minty breeze drifting through Polly's herb garden, and the salty tang blowing up from the ocean. With a sigh, she sank down into a chair and began sipping from her mug. The rhythmic sound of the waves crashing against the cliff below was like a symphony in her ears, and on any other occasion it would have soothed her like a lullaby. But she was beyond soothing tonight.

All because of Jake...

'Here.' His voice came unexpectedly out of the dark behind her, making her jump. 'I've brought you a liqueur. You took off in such a hurry, you didn't give me time to ask what you'd like, so I'm afraid you won't have a choice. I've brought you a brandy.'

The thundering of the waves had muffled the sound of his steps as he crossed the patio; Briony found herself hoping it would also conceal the tremor in her voice as she replied stiffly, 'Thank you, but I have a mug of coffee.'

'That's all right, so do I.'

Her eyes were now used to the near-dark, and since he'd thrown off his jacket after dinner it was easy to see where he was as his white shirt glimmered as he moved. She watched him warily as he placed a small tray bearing a mug of coffee and two balloon glasses on the low table... and then she drew back slightly as he sat down on a seat close to her own. Too close. Too close for comfort. The breeze carried his male scent to her, so that for the second time that evening she felt a shiver ripple through her.

What was wrong with her? she wondered bewilderedly. The musky scent of Jake's skin and hair had been familiar to her for years—forever, it seemed—but it was just part of him, and she'd never really paid it any attention before. Now, inexplicably, it disturbed her senses...

'We can add the brandy to our coffee.' His quietly spoken words broke into her scrambled thoughts. 'It'll make a pleasant end to the evening.'

'It was nice of the Denhams to come over.' Briony could hear the stiltedness in her voice.

'Diane invited you to come sailing with us—I was surprised when you said you wouldn't. Won't you change your mind? They're forecasting near-perfect weather.'

Briony had always thought Jake's voice was one of the nicest things about him. When he talked quietly, as he was doing now, it had a deep, velvety quality that was like a gentle caress. In the past, she would have closed her eyes and relaxed, enjoying the deliciously soothing sensation.

Tonight, her resentment towards him made that impossible.

'No, Jake, I won't change my mind.' Her coffee had cooled a little, and she managed to drink it all down in one go. Then, mug in hand, she got to her feet. 'Like Polly, I'm tired,' she said steadily. 'I'm going to bed. Thanks for bringing the brandy, but I'll pass. You'll remember to lock the door when you come in?'

His chair was between her and the kitchen door; she realised too late that she should have taken that into consideration. As she made to walk past him, he swiftly uncoiled himself from his seat and stood up, towering over her as he stopped her by grasping her upper arms.

His grip was in no way painful, but it was very firm. She could feel the steely imprint of each finger as it clamped against her flesh... and she knew that even if she struggled she had no chance of freeing herself. Besides, to struggle would only lower the dignity she so badly wanted to preserve. Taking in a deep breath, she looked up at him, and wasn't surprised to see a hard, determined glint in his blue eyes. Well, he might be determined... but so was she.

'Let me go, Jake.'

'You're acting like a spoiled child, Briony.' His voice, velvety-smooth a moment before, was now sandpaper-rough with impatience and frustration. 'I don't know you when you're like this. You've always been so sweet, so——'

'If I'm acting like a child, it's because you've been treating me like one. I'm surprised you've allowed me to stay up this late,' she added sarcastically. 'It's way past a child's bedtime.'

His grip tightened. 'Dammit, the last thing I wanted was to get into this again, but, if it helps any, I do know how disappointed you are about the trip. I do understand——'

'No, you don't, Jake. But, like you, the last thing I want to do is talk about it. Now I'm going to bed, so will you please allow me to leave?' There, she had achieved just the right degree of frigid disdain!

'You little idiot...' He shook her gently, and as he did the wind gusted, blowing her hair forward around her cheeks and causing it to dance in the air between them. And along with it drifted the scent of her Chanel.

She hadn't been aware of the perfume during the course of the party, but now, mingled as it was with Jake's musky male scent, and the intoxicating fragrance of the summer night, it suddenly became overpowering. Overpowering and sensual. The heady mixture infiltrated her every pore, making her dizzy. To her dismay, she felt herself swaying forward. And, to her horror, she felt the peaks of her breasts lightly brush against Jake's chest, felt his warmth, his hard power, the steady drumbeat of his heart, through his white shirt.

For the third time that night she felt a shiver ripple through her—this time so dramatically that it made her gasp. She felt Jake stiffen. But only for a moment. Then he dropped his hands from her arms as if she had suddenly become red-hot, and stepped back abruptly.

For a moment Briony didn't hear the thumping of the waves against the cliff below, or the breeze rustling through the rose bushes edging the patio. All she could hear was her own rasping breath, and the blood pounding in her ears.

Jake was the first to speak, to break the fragile tension that she could feel quivering so tremulously between them.

'You're right. It's time you were in bed.' There was a harsh command in his tone that she had never heard before, a harsh command that left her in no doubt that she'd better obey him.

But now that she was free to go she seemed, strangely, to be rooted to the spot. Try as she might, she just couldn't move. Only when Jake's insistent, 'Good*night*, Briony!' exploded in her ears did she finally regain control of her limbs. But even as she opened her mouth automatically to return his goodnight she decided against it. She wasn't sure what had happened between them a moment ago, but she knew that, whatever it was, it had been her fault, and it had caused him to erect a wall between them that hadn't been there before.

She also knew that if she tried to speak the only sound that would come out would be a squeak.

And her humiliation would be complete.

With her lips clamped tightly together to stop their trembling, she side-stepped his darkly looming figure, and stumbled back into the house.

To her amazement, despite the late cup of coffee and the turmoil of her emotions, she slept well. When she woke next morning she felt refreshed... and when she glanced at her watch and saw it was almost nine she breathed a sigh of relief. Jake would be long gone on his way to Smuggler's Cove with Diane, and she wouldn't have to face him.

After a quick shower she pulled on a white T-shirt and a pair of denim cut-offs, and, yanking her blonde hair into a pony-tail, she slid on a pair of white leather thongs and ran down to the kitchen.

A WOMAN'S LOVE

There was a note propped against the coffee-pot.

Briony—clean forgot I have a dentist's appointment at ten. I'll be back around noon. Love, Polly.

Briony chuckled, shaking her head. Poor, absent-minded Poll! One of these days she'd forget something really important, then maybe that would prompt her to get her act together!

Humming under her breath, Briony poured herself a glass of chilled orange juice, and walked to the window. The sea was a brilliant azure-blue, reflecting the clear sky. A beautiful morning, she thought, as she felt the sun's rays kiss her bare arms. It was going to be a scorcher.

She was thankful to have the whole place to herself. She had some serious thinking to do, and she didn't want to be disturbed.

But why stay indoors? she mused as she finished her juice. It was far too nice a day

Ten minutes later she was sitting on the beach, scantily clad in a bright red bikini. Leaning back against the cliff face, her toes digging into the white sand, she stared unseeingly at the vividly coloured sails of the dozen or so yachts shimmering on the horizon.

How was she going to come up with the money she needed?

She could, of course, drive into Falmouth or Bridgeport this very afternoon and look for a job. But who would hire her? She wanted to work for only four weeks—and besides, she wasn't trained for anything. She couldn't type, she didn't know how to use a computer, she had no idea how a cash register worked.

What *could* she do?

Her smile was self-derisive. All she could do was draw and paint.

She clasped her arms round her knees, frowning as she remembered something.

Remembered *somebody*.

Rhona McLeod from Skye.

Slowly, she uncapped her tube of sunscreen and began smoothing the clear gel over her arms. Rhona, a fellow student at Marwyck Art College, had returned after the summer break last year with a balance in her savings account that had made all her friends gasp with envy.

'It was the easiest thing in the world,' the freckled west-coaster had boasted. 'I dashed off hundreds of little canvases in acrylic—of the castles, the Cuillins, the fishing boats. Bright, flashy, and trashy... to sell to the tourists.' Her tone was faintly contemptuous as she went on, 'Caught them as they came off the ferry. It was like taking candy from a baby.' Snapping her bank book shut, she slid it back into her eelskin purse and grimaced. 'My old art teacher from Inverness Academy drove by one day and scolded me soundly. Said I was prostituting myself, turning out such slapdash, inferior work, in light of my talent.'

Briony had been inclined to agree. At the time. But now... She felt her pulse-rate quicken as she thought of the possibilities.

If Rhona had had an ideal situation in Skye, she, Briony, had a perfect set-up here. Devil's Crag was located midway between Falmouth and Bridgeport, on a busy scenic route that was bumper-to-bumper tourists during the summer. Tourists from all over the world, tourists eager to spend their money on unique souvenirs to take home with them.

Souvenirs that she, Briony, could provide. Souvenirs that she would be only too happy to provide.

Jake wouldn't be pleased.

The thought skipped into her mind out of nowhere. And others followed...

She had told Jake about Rhona McLeod in one of her regular letters to him, and he'd replied by return on a sheet of his law firm's thick, expensive paper, in his distinctive black scrawl.

Re your friend from Skye. I think you can guess what my comment will be. Integrity is everything, Bri. I trust that *you* will never give less than your best.

She twisted her shoulders impatiently as she recalled her emotional reaction to his words—the tears that had sprung to her eyes, her melodramatic avowal that if she were ever to let Jake down in any way, when he expected so much of her, she would never be able to forgive herself.

Claptrap!

His postcard must have caught her at a moment when her spirits were low, a moment when she was homesick for Cornwall and the Crag. There was absolutely no harm in what she was planning to do.

And, in any case, if Jake did disapprove, he had only himself to blame. With his dictatorial attitude, had he not driven her to it?

She'd go to her studio after lunch and get started. In the meantime she would take this one morning off. With a grin, she slid off her red mesh bikini-top and tossed it flippantly into the air. Then, after applying her sun-screen, she stretched out, face-down on her beach towel, and gave herself up to the pleasures of the sun.

She dozed for about half an hour, and then, as she was lazily considering turning over on to her back, she thought she heard someone whistling.

She frowned, tensing a little. But though she strained her ears for several long seconds all she could hear was the suck and gurgle of the surf on the sand and among the rocks, and the drone of a plane high up in the sky.

She must have been mistaken, she decided—or perhaps what she'd heard had been the whistle of a flighting oyster-catcher. This beach belonged to the Crag and was very private, accessible only by boat or by the steep steps, carved into the sixty-foot cliff, which led down from the kitchen patio. The boathouse where *Trelawney's Woman* was kept was around the bluff—she and Jake were the only people who ever used this particular stretch of the beach, the steps being too much for Polly now. And today Jake would already be more than halfway to Smuggler's Cove!

Relaxing again, Briony twisted round on to her back. Mm, the hazy warmth of the sun was lovely; she could feel all yesterday's tension seeping away. Like a contented kitten she stretched out her arms, and, sliding her fingers into the white sand, let the grains sift through them. Bliss, she mused, absolute——

She heard the sound again. This time it was closer at hand. Much closer at hand. Not the whistle of a sea-pie after all, but a man's whistle, absent-minded, toneless...

She jerked herself to a sitting position, and with her heart leaping into her throat, and her tousled hair swinging across her cheeks, she frantically looked around for her bikini-top. Where in heaven's name was it?

Relief surged through her as she spotted it above her head, dangling from a wiry plant on the black rock face. Scrambling to her feet, she flung herself up on her tiptoes, and was just making a second desperate try at capturing the skimpy Lycra garment when from the corner of her eye she saw a long shadow fall sideways over the cliff face.

Her gasp died in her throat as a tall, deeply tanned figure in faded navy trunks came into her line of vision.

Dear God... dismay shuddered through her... it was Jake!

CHAPTER THREE

BLACK hair dripping wet, rivulets of water running down his shoulders and into the dark curls covering his chest, Jake had obviously been swimming.

He stopped abruptly when he saw her, and, like lightning flashing in a thunderstorm, tension crackled between them with a speed and a power that took Briony's breath away and paralysed her.

But, though sanity told her she stood frozen for only a millisecond, it seemed like forever. Riveted, she gazed disbelievingly, every cell in her body screaming in protest. Jake was supposed to be on his way to Smuggler's Cove. How could he be here?

'What the *devil*...?'

His tone was so harsh, so accusing that it broke whatever spell had been immobilising her. With her mind skittering around in a mixture of confusion and panic, she sprang up and, with flailing hands, again grabbed for her bikini-top. This time she was successful, and a silent prayer of thanks breathed from her lips as she tugged the garment down with such force that the twig snapped. In one fluid movement she swivelled round so that her back was to Jake and tumbled her breasts into the red mesh cups. Then, with fingers that seemed suddenly to be all thumbs, she tied the spaghetti straps that secured it.

Why couldn't she have reacted more quickly? she asked herself angrily. Why couldn't she have snatched her bikini-top and put it on *before* Jake came round the corner? Because she'd hesitated, she'd been too late. Oh, only a minute fraction of a second too late. But during that minute fraction of a second the world had ground to a halt on its axis, and everything had seemed magnified, every minute detail crystal-clear. She had seen Jake's expression become taut, a muscle twitch convulsively in his jaw, his pupils become dilated...

And his eyes, as his incredulous gaze had encompassed her full, high breasts with their delicate fawn nipples, had held an expression she'd never seen before. A shocked, stunned expression that had left her feeling as if someone had swept her legs from under her. An expression that made her want to look anywhere but at him.

But she knew she had to turn and face him. She couldn't stand like this forever, staring blindly at the black rocks in front of her. Even if he were to walk away now, she would still have to face him eventually. Better to get it over with.

She stifled a self-deprecating exclamation. Only yesterday she'd been unbearably frustrated because it was obvious that Jake still saw her as a child. But a woman—today's woman—wouldn't have behaved the way she had just behaved. She would have been poised, calm, self-assured.

She inhaled a determined breath. She was a woman... but if she wanted to convince Jake of that she'd better start acting like one!

Gathering up every ounce of self-control she possessed, she turned round, somehow managing to curve her lips in a cool smile. 'You took me by surprise, Jake—startled me for a moment. I thought I had the beach to myself.' With a deliberately careless gesture, she brushed away a few grains of white sand clinging to her bikini-top.

'Oh, I can see I took you by surprise.' Jake's voice was icy cold. 'But your own surprise is mild compared to mine. The last thing I expected as I strolled along the beach was to come on you cavorting around half naked.'

The edge of contempt to his tone was like a tiny stab wound to Briony's heart. She had never before been subjected to Jake's disapproval, and it hurt. But the last thing she wanted was for him to know it. '*Cavorting?*' She gave a dismissive laugh. 'I wasn't cavorting, Jake. I was merely trying to get an even tan.' She saw his lips tighten into a thin line, and the sight provoked her into adding lightly, 'But surely you're used to seeing half-naked women? A man of your experience, in this day and——'

'We're not talking about me.' His voice had become even harsher, and a flare of angry colour darkened his face. 'We're talking about *you*. Don't you realise you're asking for trouble? What if it had been someone else who came on you just now? What if it had been a stranger?'

'But it wasn't someone else... it was you, wasn't it?' Briony snapped. 'And you're not a stranger, *are* you? You're my ex-guardian. If I should feel safe with anyone in the world, it should be you. And I do feel safe with you. How could I not,' she added sarcastically, 'locked as I am in the little cage you've constructed for me?'

'Sometimes a cage is necessary.' His voice had the cutting edge of a scalpel. 'And some day you may find that out for yourself. In the meantime—yes, Briony, you're safe with me. You can count on that, if you can count on nothing else in this world.'

For a long moment, they glared at each other, the air bristling with hostility, and neither one willing to give an inch. And then, with a terse, frustrated exclamation, Jake turned abruptly and strode away in the direction from which he'd come.

Immediately he disappeared from view, all the fight drained out of Briony. With legs like jelly, she slumped back against the rock face, barely aware of the rough shells scraping her skin as desolation settled over her like a shroud.

Jake had said he no longer knew her. Well, she, in turn, no longer knew him.

He was a stranger to her.

How could this have happened?

She shook her head disbelievingly as she tried to reconcile the new Jake with the compassionate Jake who had become her guardian ten years before, the Jake who had been her only rock in a world which had suddenly seemed to consist of sinking sands, a rock to which she'd found herself clinging as desperately, as stubbornly, as a limpet.

She hadn't seen much of Jake till that time, as he'd been away at university most of the year, and during his vacations he'd worked as a deck-hand on one of the supply vessels to the North Sea oil rigs. But he'd graduated as a lawyer shortly before her mother's death, and a couple of weeks afterwards had accepted an offer to article with Bridgeport's biggest law firm, and, to Briony's delight, he had come home to the Crag for good.

The relationship that had developed between them had been comfortable, and, for Briony, comforting. She had always taken for granted that it was also indestructible. Only now did she realise that it wasn't.

She felt an ache deep in her heart. Only now did she realise just how very precious that relationship had been.

Now that it was shattered.

Now that it was too late.

The sun was shining as brightly as ever, but somehow she didn't feel like staying at the beach any longer. The joy had gone out of it. Feeling as if her heart had turned to lead, she wrapped her beach towel round herself, and, scooping up her tube of sunscreen, made her way back to the house.

'So Diane had a migraine——' Polly set the salad bowl in the centre of the kitchen table '—and you had to cancel your little jaunt. That was disappointing for you, Jake.' She pulled out her chair and sat down. 'What did you do instead?'

Briony knew her cheeks had become stained with pink, and she avoided looking across the table at Jake, but she sensed that he was looking at her.

'I went for a swim.' His voice was casual. 'And then for a walk along the beach. Briony, would you like some of the cold roast, or would you prefer the chicken?'

Briony fixed her eyes on the blue and white checked gingham tablecloth as she muttered, 'I think I'll have the chicken.' As Jake passed her the platter, she made sure she took it without touching his fingers. 'Thank you.'

'And how about you, dear?' Polly patted her arm. 'You turned down the chance to go sailing—that wasn't like you! Did you have something special planned for this morning?'

Involuntarily, Briony's gaze flicked up to find that Jake was staring at her with a shuttered expression. She jerked her gaze away. 'I went down to the beach too, because I——'

'Ah.' Polly passed her the salad bowl. 'So you and Jake were together. Good. I had forgotten about my appointment, and I didn't want you to be alone.' She pushed her chair back and stood up. 'I'm going out to the patio to do a little weeding now—just pop your dishes in the dishwasher when you're done——'

'Aren't you going to have some lunch, Polly?' Jake looked up at her, frowning.

'No, Fenton filled a tooth and he told me not to chew on it for a few hours. I'll eat later.' She turned to Briony. 'There's a coconut cream pie in the fridge, dear. Don't let Jake have more than his fair share; you know what he's like when it comes to pies!' Chuckling, Polly took a pair of gardening gloves from a drawer, and disappeared through the open doorway leading to the patio.

For a few minutes there was no sound in the kitchen except for the hum of the fridge and the occasional faint scrape of cutlery against china. Then, just as Briony was swallowing the last mouthful of her chicken, Jake spoke.

'What were you going to say when Polly interrupted you?' he asked softly. 'You said you went down to the beach because...?'

Briony put down her fork, and touched her serviette to her lips. It was on the tip of her tongue to retort, Because I wanted to cavort around half naked, but she managed to bite the words back. Instead, she said calmly, 'I had some thinking to do.'

'About what?'

'I'd rather not say.' She got up and put her plate and cutlery into the dishwasher and then took the pie from the fridge.

'A secret, is it?'

His tone was teasing, and Briony knew that he was holding out an olive-branch. But she was not about to accept it.

'For the moment, yes,' she said curtly. Placing the pie-dish on the counter-top, she cut a generous slice for Jake and put it on a plate. 'There you are.' She pushed the pie across the table to him.

'Where's your own?'

'I'm not having dessert.'

'Watching your figure?'

Briony was in no doubt that as soon as he'd uttered the gently mocking words he wished them unsaid, but it was too late. They hung heavily in the air between them as their eyes locked, and Briony felt her throat muscles tighten as the memory of the morning's awkward incident slid into her mind... as it must have into his too.

'If I don't watch my figure, then nobody else will want to, will they?' she said with a cool smile.

She saw emotion flicker briefly over his face. Anger? Frustration? She wasn't sure... maybe it was a mixture of the two. But his voice gave no sign that her response had affected him in any way as he steered the conversation back to its original course. 'You'll hurt Poll's feelings, if she comes back and finds only one slice of her pie gone.'

'Then you'll just have to eat my slice for me,' she returned with saccharine sweetness. 'And I'm sure that'll be no hardship. Now, if you'll excuse me, I have things to do. If anyone wants me, I'll be in my studio.'

'Surely you're not going to work on such a beautiful day. You——'

The ringing of the phone interrupted whatever Jake had been about to say. It was a wall phone, situated by the door, and, as Briony was closer to it, automatically she lifted the handset.

'Trelawney residence.' While she spoke, Briony stubbornly challenged the lingering, dark disapproval in Jake's gaze, locking her eyes unflinchingly with his. It was none of his business whether or not she buried herself in her studio on this beautiful day... and the way she felt about him right now whatever he didn't want her to do, then that was what she *would* do!

'May I please speak to... Mr Trelawney?'

The woman's voice coming across the line dragged Briony's attention from Jake. She frowned. She didn't recognise the voice... yet there was something familiar about it—about its slight hesitancy, its soft huskiness. The unique timbre echoed its way into the deepest recesses of her mind, triggering memories, but triggering them so weakly that they floated on the periphery of her consciousness, and she could no more grasp them than she could have grasped the air stirred by a butterfly's wings.

Instead of handing the phone to Jake, she found herself giving in to her curiosity. 'May I ask who's calling?'

For a long moment there was silence on the line, except for the sound of classical music playing quietly in the background at the other end. Briony was just about to repeat her question when she heard the woman say in a breathless rush, 'Oh, if he's not at home, I can——'

'He's right here. Just a moment, please.'

At her words, Jake pushed back his chair and got up.

'Who is it?' he mouthed.

Her answering shrug told him she didn't know.

He crossed to where she was standing, and she felt her nerves tremble as his familiar musky scent reached her nostrils. Swallowing, she stepped back a little, but as he took the phone and she twisted to get past him the cord wrapped itself round her and she found herself wound against his side. His shirt-sleeves were rolled up almost to his elbow, and as her bare forearm brushed against his hair-roughened skin she felt a strange quiver shudder through her, a quiver so jolting that it made her gasp. Immediately she forced a laugh in an effort to make light of her only too obvious physical reaction to his touch... a laugh that died away slowly as she saw Jake's expression. He wasn't laughing. In fact she couldn't remember when she'd seen him look more shocked.

She felt her heart give a horrified lurch. Dear heaven, he knew. He was as aware of her reaction to his touch as *she* was... and even more appalled by it.

She could see it in his eyes.

Eyes that had become cold and distant——

'Hello... hello? Have we been cut off?'

The husky, hesitant voice drifting through the air should have stimulated Briony to draw away from Jake, but she couldn't, not if her life had depended on it. Even if the telephone cord hadn't trapped her, his raw masculinity, the devastating magnetism he emanated would have. The only things she was aware of were his lean, tanned face so close to her own, the coffee flavour of his breath as it fanned her cheeks, the hard warmth of his body.

It was he who finally severed the connection between them, jerking his gaze abruptly away from hers and flipping the cord loose so that she was no longer tangled in it. Then he turned away from her.

'Trelawney speaking.' His voice was steady, as was the hand holding the receiver.

His hands might be steady, Briony thought self-derisively, but hers weren't. Nor were her legs! Feeling as loose-jointed as a puppet, she made her way out of the kitchen, touching the back of a chair on the way for support. As she walked through the corridor towards the foyer, she muttered aloud to herself, 'Damn, damn, damn!' An idiot, that was what she was; an absolute *idiot*. Why couldn't she have more control over herself; why, in heaven's name, had she just stood there, like some besotted teenager—gazing up at him as mindlessly as if he were Richard Gere?

She paused at the foot of the stairs, gnawing her lip abstractedly. She couldn't just leave things the way they were; she had to *say* something, or *do* something to make Jake believe he'd misread her reaction to him. But what...?

As she struggled to come up with an answer, she noticed that the mail had arrived—it had been pushed through the slot in the door, and lay scattered on the slate floor. Scooping up the letters, she made to place them on the hall table, but at the last minute changed her mind, realising that they were a heaven-sent answer to her dilemma. She would take them through to the kitchen, and act so nonchalantly, so airily with Jake that if he had any suspicions about her feelings towards him they would be swiftly put to rest.

Moving purposefully back along the corridor, she pushed open the swing door again. Jake was still on the phone, and she was just in time to hear him murmur, 'I'll see you there in about an hour,' before he replaced the receiver.

Was it her imagination, or had the tension in the room tightened a few notches since she'd left a few moments ago? Jake's features were certainly more tautly drawn than they had been earlier, and now, as he watched Briony come into the kitchen, a dark frown drew down his strongly marked eyebrows. She felt a quiver of uncertainty; he was looking at her in the same way she'd caught him looking at her in the drawing-room the evening before. It was a strange look, a penetrating look, as if he knew well enough what was on the surface, but he was trying to see beneath. And if she was interpreting his expression accurately, what he was seeing presented him with some kind of a problem...

Oh, she was crazy. He was probably not seeing her at all; he was *looking* at her, but he was probably not even aware of her. He was probably letting his mind wander to his upcoming rendezvous with the woman who had just called him. The woman with the husky, slightly hesitant voice—the kind of voice Briony imagined a man would find very sexy. The kind of voice *Jake* would probably find very sexy.

She didn't know why, but the thought made her irritable. 'You're going out, then?' she said snappishly, and, with an impatient gesture, she tossed the mail on to the table. 'How fortunate for you that Diane came down with a migraine, otherwise you'd have been way out at sea when this other... friend... called, and you'd have missed her.'

If she expected Jake to lash out at her for her sarcasm, she was disappointed. He appeared not to have heard her. He dragged a hand through his hair and with a frustrated sigh turned away from her. Crossing the kitchen, he paused in the open doorway that led out to the patio garden, his back to Briony. Beyond his tall, shadowed form, she could see Polly over by the top of the cliff steps, stooping over one of her rose bushes.

When Jake finally turned to face her, his eyes were troubled. 'Briony,' he said in a low voice, 'I've been thinking... about this trip you want to take——'

'You've got it wrong, Jake. The trip I'm *going* to take.'

'I can't get away for the next few months, my caseload is too heavy, but if you can wait till the spring I'll take you to Paris, to Florence, to wherever it is you want to go. It will be my graduation present to you.'

Briony stared at him, trying to assimilate what he had just said. At first she couldn't believe her ears... but when she finally realised she had heard aright, and she was faced with the magnitude of his arrogance, she felt anger shuddering through her with such force that she thought her chest might burst.

'How can you even suggest such a thing?' she exploded. 'Have you missed the whole point of the trip? It's not just that I'm going to Paris, and Florence, and Venice—it's that I'm going with Professor Sharp! Oh, you make me so damned mad! You can find the money to take me... but you can't advance me my own money from the trust!' With a great effort, Briony managed to keep her voice from becoming shrill. 'Jake, I'd like you to get one thing straight... and then I'm not going to talk about it again. Read my lips—*I am going to Europe with the Sharps*. And——' she hurried on as he opened his mouth to speak '—even if I weren't, I wouldn't go with you. I wouldn't go anywhere with you. Not after the selfish, dictatorial way you've treated me. To tell you the truth, I wouldn't even walk across the street with you—not for all the tea in China!'

Without taking his eyes from her, Jake put a hand behind him and slammed the kitchen door. As he did so, Briony felt a quick stab of apprehension. Apprehension that increased as he crossed the space between them in three quick strides, tension apparent in every aspect of his bearing.

'You may not want to spend time in my company, but tonight you are going to, whether you like it or not——'

'Sorry, I have plans for this evening.' Briony managed to sound flippant. 'Polly and I haven't had a chance to catch up on all our news and she wants to have me all to herself tonight. I've promised to sit with her after dinner——'

'You won't be sitting with Polly tonight. You'll be sitting with me.' His lips twisted in a cold smile. 'In the Theatre by the Sea in Bridgeport.'

'You think I'd go to the *theatre* with you?' Briony's laugh was incredulous. 'After everything that's happened? After the way you've tried to *manipulate* me? No way, Jake. Didn't you hear what I just said? Wild horses couldn't drag me to the theatre with you!'

'Keep your voice down, for Pete's sake.' Jake glanced frowningly at the open window. In a lowered voice, he went on tersely, 'Polly has bought two tickets for us, for *The Pirates of Penzance*. It's supposed to be a surprise——'

'But I don't want to go out with you, Jake——'

'What you want is immaterial in this instance,' he gritted out. 'I'm warning you, when Polly produces the tickets, you make damned sure you let her think you're delighted. When her old car packed in she had to dig into her savings to buy that new Vauxhall—she can ill afford to be splurging on expensive theatre tickets!'

In the past, the prospect of an evening out with Jake *would* have delighted Briony, but now the very idea added fuel to the contempt and resentment she could feel simmering inside her... But she didn't need the brain of an Einstein to see that she was trapped.

'I'd never do anything to upset Polly. As you well know.' She managed to twist her lips into a mocking smile as she spun on her heel and began stalking to the door. 'So it seems,' she threw over her shoulder regally, 'that we're going to be stuck with each other for the evening.'

'Yes, I'm afraid we are. By the way,' his voice echoed coolly after her as she pushed open the swing door and stalked away along the corridor, 'I won't be home for dinner—but don't worry, I'll be back in good time.'

He really hadn't needed to add that, Briony thought resentfully—Jake was never late for an appointment, so he wouldn't keep her waiting, no matter how much he might be tempted to dally with his mysterious caller.

Who *was* she, anyway?

Briony uttered an exclamation of exasperation as she crossed the hall to the front door. How irritating it was, to have half recognised the woman's voice! There was no doubt that the fragile memory would niggle away at her tantalisingly till it finally surfaced. If it ever did!

Of course, she could always ask Jake tonight who it was he'd gone out to meet.

But the caller had avoided giving her name...and Jake might refuse to do so too. She certainly didn't want to risk giving him that satisfaction!

Briony's studio was at the top of the cliff, about two hundred yards from the house and partially screened from it by hydrangea bushes. The square cement building had once been a garage, but Jake had found its location inconvenient, especially after Polly had come to stay at the Crag. On winter nights, when she'd parked her car there after coming back around ten from her gardening club meetings, she'd had to find her way to the house in the dark, and despite her insistence that she could manage Jake was even more insistent that he wouldn't tolerate it. And so he had a new garage built just yards from the back door. The old garage had sat unused for the next four years till Jake had seen that Briony intended to make art her career, and he'd had it converted into a studio. It consisted of one large, north-facing room, with two cupboards, and a long, scarred oak bench running under an enormous plate-glass window.

She loved it. It was the place she felt most at home in the whole world.

And after her altercation with Jake in the kitchen she went straight there.

The place hadn't been in use since the Christmas break and she found a layer of dust over everything. She had just cleared everything off the bench, and was rummaging in the drawer for a duster, when from the corner of her eye she noticed a movement outside, and, distracted, she glanced out of the uncurtained window.

Through a gap in the hydrangea bushes she saw Jake striding from the house towards his silver Jaguar. He was wearing an open-necked shirt and jeans, and he had a heathery tweed sports jacket slung over one shoulder.

Briony leaned forward, rubbing the grime from the sun-warmed glass with her fingertips so that she could see better. And as her eyes took in Jake's tall, rangy frame, and the masculine grace with which he moved, an indefinable ache gently squeezed her heart, and for a moment she forgot all the harsh words that had passed between them.

Why, she wondered confusedly, did she feel such an odd sense of loss? She should have been glad he was going to be away all afternoon, for she could anticipate a few hours of peace and quiet... but instead she felt... restless.

Was it because this glorious afternoon reminded her of the many summer afternoons she and Jake had spent roaming the moors together in the past? Or... was it because he was going to be spending this particular afternoon with the owner of the soft and very sexy voice?

As the gravel churned under the Jaguar's rear wheels and the powerful vehicle shot away along the drive, Briony roughly tugged a duster from the drawer, and began running it vigorously along the top of the bench. What Jake did was of no interest to her! She had her own life to think about. Her goal was to make enough money by the end of the month to go on her trip, and she wasn't going to achieve it if she stood gazing out of her studio window! Resolutely, she swept all thoughts of him from her mind, and set to work.

She cleaned till around three o'clock, and then began making up the list of things she would need for her money-making project. When she totalled up the approximate cost of the necessary supplies a whistle escaped her lips. If she'd needed just one or two canvases, she'd have shopped at McNabb's in Bridgeport, but the dozens of small canvases she'd require, plus all her other purchases, would necessitate a trip to Artist's Lo-Cost Centre in Falmouth; their competitive prices would make the extra journey well worthwhile. She'd drive there first thing tomorrow——

'Why on *earth* are you indoors on such a gorgeous day?'

Briony swivelled her head round and saw Polly standing in the open doorway, gardening basket over her arm, white daisies trailing from it, and a small trowel in her hand.

'Why, you're filthy!' Jake's aunt went on before Briony could reply. 'You're absolutely covered in dust and cobwebs! What——?'

'I've been spring-cleaning, Poll—belatedly!' Briony flung out one grimy hand in a wide gesture. 'The studio looks nice, doesn't it?'

Polly glanced round. 'Mm, it does, dear.' Her roving gaze came to rest on an arrangement of about twenty pen and ink drawings thumb-tacked to one of the white-washed walls. Moving over to examine the finely detailed sketches, she said warmly, 'I'm so glad you've kept these, Briony; of all the work you've done in the past, they are my favourites.'

Briony strolled over to join her, smiling reminiscently as she looked at the very intricate drawings. 'Mine too. I can remember when I did the first one—I was thirteen, and I'd just begun taking a sketch-pad with me every time I walked on the moors. On this particular day I was on my way home when suddenly I got the feeling someone was watching me, and as I glanced round I caught sight of this rather scraggy fox——' she indicated one of the sketches '—squinting at me from behind a hedge. He looked so comical, I just had to draw him. And when I finished the first rough draft I realised I'd dressed him in an old raincoat and a felt hat, like the detective on that TV show you love to watch.'

'And that started it!' Polly chuckled. 'I like the raven best, with his pirate's hat and the black patch over his eye. But of course the bee is wonderful too, buzzing around the escallonia with his chain-saw...'

'It took me ages to do each one, but it was worth it.'

As she spoke the words, Briony felt her conscience twingeing. She knew she wasn't going to reap the same sort of satisfaction from the work she was intending to do this summer! Shrugging away the unwelcome thought, she changed the subject, saying lightly, 'I'll have to come to the kitchen to borrow your window-cleaner, Polly, but everything else is shipshape. You know me—I can't work in a mess.'

Polly twisted round to face her. '*Work*?' Her tone was scandalised. 'Dear, what you need is a holiday—and I want you to have one before I go away——'

'Away? Where are you going, Poll?'

'My god-daughter Kate asked if I'd look after her two wee ones when she goes into hospital to have her baby...'

'Oh, yes, you mentioned that in one of your letters— it slipped my mind. She's due in late July, isn't she?'

'Mm. I'll be away for at least a week. I want to make sure Kate has a good rest when she comes home. And that's what you need, dear—a good rest, plus lots of home cooking. And...' her eyes twinkled mischievously '...a bit of fun. I'm a great believer in the old saying, "Laughter is the best medicine"...'

Briony guessed what Polly was leading up to. She had a fleeting image of Jake and herself driving in hostile silence to the theatre, but she managed to say with a lightness she was far from feeling, 'You're right, Poll. I did take my finals very seriously. I shall really have to make more of an effort now to relax but I'm afraid I've got out of the habit!' She threw her hands out in front of her in a helpless gesture. 'Where on earth do I start?'

It was all she could do to keep her face straight as she saw Polly's cheeks turn bright pink with excitement. 'I know exactly where you can start!' The older woman dug deeply into the pocket of her gardening smock, and, drawing out two green tickets, waggled them in front of Briony gleefully. 'These are for you and Jake, dear, for tonight. For *The Pirates of Penzance*, at the Theatre by the Sea. A little surprise! I didn't mean to tell you till——'

She got no further as Briony gave her a hug that squeezed the breath from her small body. 'Oh, Poll, how super—what a treat that'll be!'

'You can wear your new dress——'

'Oh, Poll—I tried it on; it's far too small.' Briony felt her heart sink as she recalled how ghastly she had looked in the childish frock—but she had decided Diane might be offended if she exchanged it for one in a different style, so... 'I'll see if Ellie Jasmine has one in a bigger size, next time I'm in Falmouth.' And she'd force herself to appear in it once or twice at the Folly, then it would spend the rest of its life hanging dismally in her wardrobe...

'I do hope Ellie has another the same,' Polly murmured. 'Now, dear, about your holiday...'

Briony moved to the sink, and, with her back to Polly, washed her hands. Jake's aunt would, of course, find out eventually about the professor's invitation, but was it necessary to tell her now? No, Briony decided, it was not. And it wasn't only unnecessary, it would be foolish, for if Polly knew she'd only become involved in the discord between herself and Jake—discord that had nothing to do with her, and would only upset her.

Briony turned, and, wiping her palms on the seat of her shorts, said reassuringly, 'Don't worry, Polly, I *am* going to take a break—in August. But I want to earn some extra spending money before then by painting and selling my work to the tourists.'

'Oh, what a good idea!' Polly nodded approvingly. 'You'll take your canvases to Roy's?'

Briony felt herself cringe inside as Polly mentioned Bridgeport's most prestigious art gallery. Clifford Roy wouldn't be interested in the kind of work she was intending to churn out! 'No,' she said, 'I don't think so. I thought it'd be easier to post a sign at the end of the lane when I have enough canvases ready, and sell them from the studio.'

Polly didn't respond right away, and in the silence Briony could hear crows cawing raucously in the woods near by. She bit her lip as she waited for Polly to speak.

At last the other woman did. Her brow pleated into a frown, she said thoughtfully, 'Does *Jake* know, dear?'

Briony hoped Polly wouldn't notice the quick rush of colour to her cheeks. 'No, I haven't mentioned it to him yet.'

'Oh.' There was another silence, even longer this time, and then Polly nodded slowly. 'I should, dear,' she said, her voice gentle, 'before you go any further with your plans. You know how much Jake values his privacy. He might not relish the idea of strangers milling around the place. It's not that he's selfish—that he's *never* been, as we both well know!—but he seems to be under a lot of strain at the moment. Of course, he never talks about his work, but lately he's been unusually distracted...I think he must be involved in a case that's worrying him. So when he's home it's especially important that he has a chance to unwind.'

Polly turned and went back outside. She stood for a moment on the stoop. Without looking round again she said, 'He won't be home for dinner, but you could ask him later how he feels about your plans—when you're at the theatre. He's been looking forward to the show—he's always been a Gilbert and Sullivan fan.'

As she moved away down the path, she called back over her shoulder, 'That's your best bet, dear. Ask him tonight. He's sure to be in a receptive mood!'

CHAPTER FOUR

JAKE wasn't.

He was in the foulest mood imaginable!

As they drove along the main street of Bridgeport, Briony sneaked a sideways look at Jake's grim profile, and knew that tonight was *not* the night to advise him of what she wanted to do. Perhaps she'd tell him tomorrow—perhaps not. Whatever, she decided as Jake swung the Jag so violently into the car park that she winced, she'd ask Polly to keep it a secret until she found the right moment.

The Theatre by the Sea was a small circular building with a tented roof, situated at the opposite end of town from Jake's law offices. It was very exclusive, and tickets cost the earth. Wine was served to patrons not only during the intermission, but also in the foyer during the half-hour before the curtain went up. This socialising was an integral part of the evening—a part which Briony was dreading. The last thing she wanted to do was stand around trying to make small talk with Jake when he was obviously in such a difficult frame of mind.

They might as well have been two strangers, she reflected bleakly as she waited for him to come back from the bar with their wine, for all the conversation that had taken place between them since leaving the Crag. The evening had started out badly, and had gone downhill from then on.

When she had come down the stairs, Jake had been restlessly pacing the hallway, immaculately dressed in silver-grey flannels and navy blazer. At sight of him, she had felt her heartbeats give an erratic kick, and she had come to an abrupt halt. She had never looked at Jake before as a woman would look at a man—speculatively, assessingly. Now, to her dismay, she found she was doing just that... and also finding that her gaze was clinging to him as if it had a mind of its own—clinging to his wide shoulders, his powerful thighs, his hard-muscled chest under his crisp white shirt.

She watched, breath caught in her throat, as he tugged impatiently at the knot of his red and navy Paisley tie. Why had she never realised before just how disturbingly attractive he was? Was it because she hadn't seen him in so long and it was like looking at a stranger? Was it because the conflict between them had caused her to view him in a new light? Whatever the reason, she couldn't deny his sexual magnetism, a magnetism that seemed to be tugging the very heart from her body.

Jake Trelawney. She shook her head unhappily. She didn't know him any more. He was no longer the comfortable, comforting Jake she'd been familiar with for years, the man who had been her guardian. Her protector. Her rock. He was a different Jake. A dark, lean, arrogant stranger.

Every woman's dream.

A little sound escaped her throat as the involuntary thought flashed into her mind, and though she tried to choke it back she was too late.

Jake must have heard it, because he jerked his head round and looked up. She saw his gaze flicker over her—over her carefully brushed hair, her sleeveless cream sheath dress, her bare, tanned legs and her flat cream leather pumps. She'd worn no jewellery, no make-up, no perfume. She had dressed as simply as she knew how. The evening was going to be hard enough to get through without running the risk of having Jake wonder contemptuously if she'd 'dolled herself up' in an attempt to attract him.

He looked at her for a long moment, and as he did he lowered his brows in a frown and his features tightened. Briony felt a trembling uncertainty. Something was wrong. Cheeks suddenly warm, she glanced down at her dress, and smoothed her hands awkwardly over her slender hips.

'Am I...suitably dressed?' Dear heavens, she sounded as shy and gawky as she'd been on her arrival at the Crag as a little girl!

He twisted away and wrenched open the door. 'Yes,' he said harshly. 'You're suitably dressed.' Jerking his head towards the forecourt outside, he added in a rough tone she barely recognised, 'Come on, dammit—let's get going!'

She knew she'd upset him but she didn't know what she'd done. And he didn't enlighten her. He slammed her door after ushering her into the passenger seat of the Jag, and once the sleek vehicle was under way he sank into a dark, brooding silence—a silence which remained unbroken till they were actually inside the theatre foyer. And then he had spoken only to ask her tersely what she wanted to drink.

She glanced at her watch as she waited for him to come back. Only a quarter to eight. Another fifteen minutes to endure the tension clashing between them, a tension which surely would dissipate once the show started. Or was Jake going to achieve the impossible, and sit through *The Pirates of Penzance* without even one chuckle?

'Briony—it *is* you! God, imagine running into you here—it's my lucky night!'

Briony blinked as a familiar male voice interrupted her thoughts, but she'd hardly had time to recognise the man who was grinning down at her—an absolutely gorgeous hunk of a man with a mass of dark blond hair hanging almost to his shoulders and eyes as green as *crème de menthe*—when he had gathered her up in a bear hug and whirled her right off her feet.

'Tony!' she gasped, as he put her down. 'I thought you were going up to Scotland to look for a job——'

He planted a kiss squarely on her lips—a kiss that tasted of garlic—and then held her away from him, his eyes crinkling. 'I decided to take a camping trip to

Cornwall first. I've always meant to, but somehow never got around to it. My forebears came from this neck of the woods and I thought I'd explore some of the old cemeteries, see if I can find any family headstones. Bridgeport looked like a good place to stay for tonight, and I was cruising the streets looking for a B and B... when I thought I saw you going up the front steps of the theatre. I parked my van and——'

'Aren't you going to introduce me to your friend, Briony?'

As Jake's cool voice interrupted, Tony looked round questioningly. When he saw Jake, he said, 'I'm sorry, sir...' He glanced at Briony. 'This your dad, love?'

Involuntarily, Briony glanced at Jake, and stifled a 'Damn!' when she saw the expression on his face. He'd been looking grim all evening; now he looked positively glacial. Thrusting Briony's wine glass at her, he raked a contemptuous glance over Tony—over the unfastened black denim shirt which contrasted so sharply with the matt of blond hair curling over his chest, over the blue jeans bleached by time and too many washings and so snug that they revealed more than they really should have——

'No, Tony,' Briony rushed in to break the tension. 'This is Jake Trelawney, my guar—my *ex*-guardian.' She took a huge gulp of her wine and watched Tony extend a hand in greeting. 'Jake, this is Tony Price, one of my friends from Marwyck College.'

'Good evening, Price.' Each of Jake's words sounded as if it had been chipped from a glacier, and his handshake—if it could be called a handshake, Briony decided with growing anger—was so brief that it should have been included in the *Guinness Book of Records*.

Tony had obviously noticed Jake's boorish behaviour too. He turned to Briony with a what-the-devil's-*his*-problem expression in his eyes, and, to smooth over the awkward moment, she said quickly, 'How long are you going to be in the area, Tony?'

'A week or so.' His grin returned. 'I knew you lived around here somewhere but I didn't have your address. Shall I pop in and pay you a visit?'

'That would be super! And why don't you plan on staying a night?' Briony added impulsively. 'There's a perfect spot for camping at the top of the cliff—just by my studio. We can have a swim together before breakfast.'

'Sounds great! I'll make a point of calling in on my way back next week.'

'Good! I'll look forward to——'

Briony's words erupted into an outraged gasp as Jake gripped her arm with fingers that seemed to gouge right into the bone.

'If you'll excuse us——' he took her glass from her fingers before she had time to resist, and deposited it on a window-sill beside his own '—we should be finding our seats. It's almost curtain time. Goodnight, Price.'

Briony saw the bewildered look in Tony's eyes, and she felt a wild surge of anger. What the devil *was* the matter with Jake? She had never known him to be so rude! With an exclamation of protest, she tried to jerk her arm free, but she might as well have tried to wrench it from the jaws of a pitbull.

'Will you stop it?' she hissed. 'Let me go!'

As if he hadn't heard her, he manoeuvred her forcefully away from Tony and towards the door leading from the foyer into the main body of the theatre. She could see several people looking their way, see several pairs of raised eyebrows. She ignored them. Over the crowd she called out to Tony before his familiar face was lost to sight. 'Devil's Crag, Tony—the second turn-off to the left after you pass Whitstable Tor——'

The rest of her words were drowned out by the sound of the orchestra and seconds later the usher was sweeping them down the centre aisle. By the time Briony was ensconced in her plush green padded seat, with a programme in her hand, the anger that had been simmering inside her was boiling over.

'Have you gone completely *crazy*?' Her words erupted up at Jake as he made to sit down. 'What the hell happened to your manners? I've never seen such appalling behaviour! Not to mention that I wanted to talk to Tony and——'

'You didn't come here to talk to Price.' He settled himself beside her, sliding his long legs around under the seat in front of him before he found a spot where he could stretch them out. 'And you didn't come here to make an exhibition of yourself. You came here to see the show.' There was a dismissive, snapping sound as he flicked open his programme. Then, drawing a spectacle case from the breast pocket of his blazer, he withdrew a pair of rimless half-glasses and put them on, then proceeded to give the programme his full attention, shutting Briony out as if she didn't exist.

Rude, uncivilised *pig*! But even as Briony's fury flared to new heights she couldn't help noticing Jake's glasses. She'd never known him to wear glasses before, and she wondered when he'd started using them. She had to admit they suited him... made him look even more intimidatingly intelligent than ever, if that were possible! The thought inexplicably added fuel to the fire burning inside her.

'You're livid because Tony thought you were my father,' she taunted. 'It stung your male ego, your pride, that he thought you were old enough to have a daughter of twenty-two.'

Jake read for a few moments before raising his eyes from the programme. Then, with his lips twisted in a cynical smile, he looked over his half-glasses at her. 'Why would that bother me, Briony? I *am* old enough to have a daughter of twenty-two. Surely you know that... or did you skip all your biology classes in high school?'

Briony lowered her eyes to avoid having to look at the ironic glitter in his. Of course, he was right. At fourteen it *would* have been physically possible for him to have——

All her thoughts crashed to a halt as she looked at his programme...the programme in which he appeared again to be so totally engrossed. She swallowed...hard. Oh, dear heavens... He couldn't possibly be reading it.

It was upside-down.

She swivelled her gaze away, an odd panic trembling through her. Straightening her back, she sat upright in her seat, her distraught gaze fixed unseeingly on the apple-green velvet curtains hanging in graceful folds to the stage. When Jake had looked at her a moment ago—cynical, arrogant, mocking—he'd seemed perfectly in control, as always. But it was a front.

She hadn't realised just how much she had upset him.

And she hadn't guessed how it would throw *her* off-balance to see *Jake* thrown off-balance. But what had she been guilty of? Just greeting an old friend with perhaps a little too much exuberance!

Why on earth should that upset Jake so much?

The question swirled around in Briony's mind, but before she could even begin to come up with an answer the lights started to dim, and the green velvet curtain swished gently upwards.

With a bewildered shake of her head, she leaned back in her seat. She'd always thought she understood the workings of Jake's mind. Only now did she realise that what went on in that complex brain of his was a complete mystery to her!

'Just a minute, Bri...'

Briony tensed as she heard Jake's voice behind her. What could he possibly want? They hadn't exchanged two civil words all evening and now that they were back at the Crag he'd decided they should *talk*? With a frustrated sigh, she turned to wait for him at the foot of the front steps. She heard him slam the car door, and seconds later he loomed out of the dark, his tall figure illuminated by the rays from the outside light.

'Yes?' she said. It was a beautiful night but cool, and as she looked up at him defensively she clasped her bare arms around herself.

'Before we go inside——' Jake's voice was weary '—I'd like to suggest a cease-fire. Polly's going to be waiting up to hear how we enjoyed the show, and if we go in like this she's going to think we've been to a funeral, instead of the theatre!'

For a moment, accusations trembled on Briony's lips. You're the one at fault, Jake, she wanted to cry. Polly gave us a warm, thoughtful, and generous gift, and you squandered it with your appalling behaviour! But she bit the words back. Polly was the one who would be hurt if she refused to go along with his suggestion. 'All right, Jake,' she said quietly, 'a cease-fire it is.'

'Good girl.' He spoke in a terse tone, but the hostility that had been there earlier had entirely disappeared. Briony thought she even detected a hint of relief, and to her surprise she felt her anger at him suddenly dissipate. His behaviour *had* been atrocious... but it had also been uncharacteristic. Was there a reason for this new Jake, the Jake who had become a stranger to her? Had she been too ready to condemn him? Should she instead have been trying to find out if there were, perhaps, problems in his life of which she wasn't aware?

He walked past her up the steps and as he fumbled under the mat for the large key Briony lingered where she stood, despite the cool wind. Why had life become so difficult? she wondered sadly, staring up at the heavens as if to find an answer there. But the vast indigo expanse offered no answer... only a million bright, twinkling stars. The Milky Way, the Plough, the Seven Sisters, Orion and his sword of gold...

The low, churring cry of a nightjar came to her on the breeze, the sound bringing memories of other nights, warm summer nights, when, as a child, she'd stood on these steps with Jake, eagerly absorbing her first lessons in astronomy. She shivered, and only then realised that he had come back down the steps and was standing beside her.

'You're cold,' he murmured. 'Here——' Taking off his blazer, he arranged it over her bare shoulders despite her little protest. 'Put this on...'

Briony felt a flush rise to her cheeks as she grasped the lapels. It was an intimate thing, to wear a man's jacket... It still held the heat from Jake's body, and the warm silk lining felt like a caress on the smooth, cool skin of her arms. His male, musky scent clung to the expensive navy nap fabric, and it rose relentlessly to her nostrils, the effect heady, intoxicating, sensual. Jerkily, she tightened her grip on the lapels as a strange yearning sensation assailed her heart. But a yearning for what...?

'So...' his steady voice broke into her thoughts '...you still enjoy star-gazing?'

Briony struggled to control her dangerously drifting emotions. 'Mm.' She cursed the slight huskiness in her tone. 'But doesn't everyone? I guess it's the mystery——'

'Look——' One of Jake's arms was suddenly, casually, around her shoulders, the other flung westward as he pointed. 'A falling star!'

She turned to follow the flight of the star, and as she did Jake's arm tightened, steadying her, and she found herself in the half-circle of his embrace, one small hand— still gripping the lapel of his jacket—trapped against his muscled chest.

The stars, the sky, the beauty of the night were all forgotten. In their place surged awareness of the man holding her—awareness of the weight of his arm around her shoulder, awareness of the pressure of his thigh against her hip, awareness of the drumming of his heart against the back of her hand—and the vague yearning she'd felt moments before crystallised with shattering swiftness to a sweet desire. All she wanted at that moment was for Jake to hold her close, hold her forever...

'Wish a wish, Bri,' he said softly.

I already have, she could have said...but she didn't. 'You too, Jake,' she managed, unable to meet his eyes.

'My wish?' Gently he smoothed her hair back from her brow and there was no hesitation in his answer. 'I wish I could keep you always safe, Bri.'

His arm tightened around her shoulder, and involuntarily Briony half turned so that she was leaning into him. It seemed natural to slide her arms round his waist, rest her cheek against his chest. His back was tautly muscled; she could feel its corded strength beneath her fingertips. A deep sigh escaped her lips. It felt so right to be in his embrace, to feel his lips touch her hair, tenderly, lovingly——

No, she must have imagined the gentle caress. His fingers were relentlessly hard as they grasped her arms and put her away from him. Startled by the unexpectedness, the abruptness of his move, she looked up, wide-eyed, to find that his gaze was darkly hooded, his expression unreadable.

'I think——' his voice had a rough texture '—it's time we went in. Poll will have heard the car—she'll be wondering what's keeping us.'

Lord, she'd done it again, Briony thought with a sinking of her heart as she followed him slowly up the steps: she'd unintentionally revealed that she found him physically attractive. And again he'd shown her, only too clearly, that her attraction to him was unwelcome.

Thank heaven Polly would be waiting for them! The presence of Jake's aunt would help smooth over the awkward tension between them.

But Polly wasn't waiting.

Instead there was a sheet of white paper propped against the phone on the hall table. Frowning, Jake picked it up, saying absently, 'My glasses, Bri...'

'Oh.' Briony slipped off his jacket and took his spectacles case from the breast pocket. As he took the case from her with a casual, 'Thanks,' he glanced at her briefly, and if he noticed the bright flush of embarrassment on her cheeks he made no sign of it. It was obvious he'd already dismissed the awkward moment from his mind. Relieved, she decided she'd better try to do the same...

Slipping on the half-glasses, Jake began reading. 'Poll's gone to Markthorpe,' he murmured, 'to look after Kate's two rascals. Kate's gone into labour and——'

Briony paused in the middle of hanging Jake's jacket in the hall cupboard. 'But her baby wasn't due till the end of the month!' she exclaimed.

'Change of plan! Ron called this evening just after we left, wanting Polly to come right away. He drove over for her so she wouldn't have to make the journey on her own.' Jake scanned the rest of the note. 'She's written a list of instructions about the casseroles and pies she has stock-piled in the freezer, and reminds you that Enoch will be here on Thursday with fresh brown eggs, and could you please water her plants?

'Well——' he laid his glasses down by the phone '—we're on our own. How about a nightcap to finish off the evening?' His voice was casual, even friendly.

About to turn down the invitation, but in an equally casual, friendly tone, Briony hesitated. She had promised herself she'd ask him tonight about using the studio; he was presenting her with an opportunity too good to turn down.

'Mm, sounds good.' She followed him into the drawing-room and sat down in an armchair by the hearth. 'Brandy for me, please.'

While he filled two fragile glasses from a bottle of Courvoisier, she found her gaze drawn irresistibly to watch him, to watch his muscular shoulders rippling under his white shirt, the shirt that contrasted so strongly, so attractively with his blue-black hair. And as her gaze dropped to the powerful thrust of his thighs, sheathed in the tightly fitting grey flannels, to her horror she felt the slow heat of desire begin to smoulder inside her again. Felt the flicker of its flame race along her veins, felt it spread a burning path across her skin, felt it ignite a thousand tiny fires in every cell, every nerve-ending...

'There you go.'

She blinked and found that he was standing in front of her.

It was impossible to take the small glass from him without touching his fingers. As skin brushed skin, Briony felt electricity spark between them, sending excitement splintering through her.

She had read about this 'electricity', this chemistry. She had thought it a flowery exaggeration, had decided—with more than a little scorn—that nothing of the sort could possibly exist outside the fantasy world of fiction. She'd been wrong. It did exist. It was powerful, sizzling, paralysing.

And she didn't want any part of it.

With a supreme effort, she forced herself to close her mind to it—and if Jake had noticed her dizzied reaction he made no sign of it.

'So...' he moved to the fireplace and leaned with lazy grace against the mantelpiece '...what are your plans for tomorrow?'

'I have a couple of things to do in Falmouth. I thought I'd drive there right after breakfast——'

'I have an appointment there at nine-thirty. We'll go to town together, no point in using two cars.'

It was on the tip of Briony's tongue to say she'd prefer to go on her own, but what was the point? Jake would just think she was being difficult. 'Fine,' she murmured.

'Now... we haven't really had time to talk since you came home. Tell me about your finals, Bri. Were they as hard as you expected?'

Staring at the rim of her glass, Briony ran an index finger round it. 'Not too bad, actually. In fact, when I came out after sitting the last paper, I felt "quietly confident", as they say. Though when Professor Sharp invited me round to his house I must admit I was apprehensive—I thought I'd somehow made a botch of everything and he wanted to let me down gently by giving me the bad news himself—but of course, when I got there, I——'

'You went to his *house*?'

The harshness of Jake's voice was so unexpected that Briony felt her heartbeats jar together alarmingly. Jerking her head up, she stared at him, and bewilderment flooded through her when she saw the angry glitter in his eyes, the dark flush that had surged to his cheeks.

'What on earth's the matter?' she asked incredulously. 'He only wanted to——'

'To *what*?' he demanded savagely.

Briony noticed that he no longer stood in his former relaxed pose; he had placed his glass on the mantelpiece, his body was rigid, and his hands were clenched tightly. He looked like someone bracing himself to fight, Briony thought, her mind reeling in confusion.

'He only wanted to invite me to go on the art trip with him.' Her voice was higher than before, and though she tried to keep it steady it trembled. 'But let's not get into *that* again!'

'You're very protective of your professor! You *admire* him, Bri?'

Protective of Professor Sharp? Why on earth would Jake think she was protective of him? 'To respond to your first comment, I don't know why you should imagine Professor Sharp requires protection, Jake,' she retorted. 'He's a brilliant man, and widely respected. And I think that answers your question. Of course I admire him.' She really hadn't meant to say more, but on a sudden impulse, out of a desire to hit out at Jake—she wasn't sure why—she added softly, 'Not only because of his talent, but because he's everything a man should be. You could learn a thing or two from him, Jake.'

For a moment, Jake froze. Then she saw him close his eyes briefly, watched with a ghastly sinking sensation as his features twisted harshly, his face took on a bloodless look. Never had she expected her cruel little gibe to cause such a reaction. Desperately wishing the insulting words unsaid...but too late...she stared numbly as he spun away from her and strode across to the cocktail cabinet. There, with jerky movements, he poured himself a large Scotch. And there, as she watched, he tilted his head and gulped the liquor down in one shuddering swallow.

Shakily, she got to her feet, and her fingers trembled as she laid her empty glass on the coffee-table. This, she knew beyond the shadow of a doubt, would not be the right time to ask him about the studio.

It would, however, be a good time to say goodnight!

'I'm off to bed, then, Jake,' she said in a rush. 'I'll see you at breakfast——'

'Not so fast!'

Jake crashed his glass on to the silver tray beside the Scotch bottle, and strode across the room to where she was standing. His features were still twisted tautly, but his face was no longer so pale. Colour again tinged his cheekbones, and his blue eyes were dark as midnight. He grasped her by the upper arms and said in a tortured voice, 'There's something you have to——'

Again, as he had done a moment before, he closed his eyes, and with a shuddering breath he dropped her arms.

'Something I have to...what, Jake?'

He opened his eyes, and looked straight down into the depths of hers. She felt dismay ripple through her as she saw the turmoil in his.

He turned away. 'Forget it,' he said tautly. 'Just forget it.'

'Forget it?' she demanded in a shaken voice. 'Forget what? How can I forget...something you haven't said?'

'Something I can't say...'

His voice was so low that she wasn't sure if she'd heard aright. 'Jake,' she asked, her own voice reedy, 'what...what was that?'

He didn't answer...and she knew by the rigid set of his wide shoulders that, no matter how long she waited, he wouldn't.

Swallowing the huge lump that was threatening to block her throat, she hesitated for a long moment, and then moved wearily across to the door. What on earth was wrong? she wondered, as she forced her trembling legs to carry her across the hall and up the stairs. Jake, usually so calm, so steady, was showing signs of stress, signs she'd never seen in him before.

Was she the cause of it?

She had a feeling that she was. Yet hadn't Polly suggested that he might be involved in a particularly difficult case? Perhaps that was the answer. Perhaps that was the reason for his frighteningly erratic behaviour.

But her instincts told her it wasn't. Her instincts told her that the reason was to do with her trip. Every time it was mentioned, he seemed to lose control. He'd made no secret of the fact that he didn't want her to go...yet it wasn't the actual trip that he was against—hadn't he offered to take her himself, if she waited till the spring?

'Sometimes a cage is necessary.'

Out of nowhere the words he'd uttered on the moor, and the scalpel-sharp tone in which they'd been delivered, came back to her, and as they did she dug her teeth deeply into her lower lip. Of course, that must be the answer. Why hadn't she realised it before? It should have been staring her in the face, in view of the way he'd been treating her since she came back from Marwyck. He didn't want her to go on the trip because he didn't trust the Sharps to look after her.

The only person who could do that job, he had obviously decided in his blind arrogance, was the one who had been doing it ever since her mother died. Himself.

Hadn't he just told her minutes ago that his wish was to keep her always safe?

Yes, he had kept her safe all these years, in the cage he'd constructed, but because she'd been happy in it she had never noticed the bars. Now, however, she could see them, and she found them unbearably confining. It was time to burst open the door and taste freedom.

And no one, not even Jake, was going to stop her!

Next morning he was withdrawn and tense, and they breakfasted together in silence. Conversation during the drive into Falmouth was almost non-existent, neither of them mentioning the events of the night before, though Briony knew that they were responsible for the tension in the air.

She was thankful when, having arranged to pick her up outside the Jasmine Boutique two hours later, he dropped her off and she was alone. Things between them couldn't get any worse, she decided grimly, as she made her way along the main street to Lo-Cost Supplies.

But when it came time for him to pick her up she realised she'd been wrong.

She had thought it would be a simple matter of exchanging the blue dress for another in the next size, but when she'd introduced herself to Ellie Jasmine and told her what she wanted Ellie had explained gently that at Jasmine Boutique the dresses were one of a kind.

'We want to ensure that our clientele will never bump into anyone else wearing a dress identical to one they have bought here! But don't worry, I'm sure we can find something else to suit you.' She scrutinised Briony with astute eyes, and as she did she frowned. 'How...strange. I thought, from the way Diane Denham described you, that you were just a little teenager. This dress——' she took the silk garment from the folds of tissue paper

'—is far too young for you...not your style at *all*, is it?'

'No——' Briony's smile was rueful '—it isn't.' She breathed up a silent prayer of thanks that here at last was someone who could see she wasn't a child!

Ellie stared at her, one index finger supporting her chin. 'I think...' She murmured a few words that were unintelligible to Briony, and then with a satisfied, 'Ah, yes!' she spun on her heel and disappeared into the nether regions of the shop.

When she came back she was holding out a slim-fitting calf-length stretch velvet dress in a leopard print, with a thigh-high slit up one side.

'Try this. It's your size. I've been keeping it in the back, waiting for just the right person.' She patted Briony's arm as she led her to a luxurious dressing-room. 'Now don't hide in here...come out as soon as you have it on...and stun me!' Ellie swished the curtain shut behind her, calling, 'Fortunately the dress is exactly the same price as the one Diane bought you!'

It might have been the same price, Briony thought several minutes later as she stared incredulously at her reflection in the mirror, but the two dresses were as different as chalk and cheese. This leopard-print outfit clung to her like a second skin, accentuating her tiny waist, the feminine curve of her hips, and the voluptuous swell of her high breasts. In addition, the colours made her fair skin look almost translucent, made her grey eyes with their long brown lashes look absolutely huge. Wow, she whispered to herself in awe, what a dress!

Only one thing was needed, she decided, to complete the picture. Bending her head forwards, she shook it violently so that her long hair fell into disarray. Then, bringing her head up sharply, she pushed the tumbled locks away from her small face, giving herself a tousled, just-out-of-bed look. Kicking off her shoes, she ran her hands over her sleek hips and murmured in disbelief.

The transformation was absolutely incredible. Where was the Briony she knew? The woman gazing back at her looked wild, sultry, alluring...

And sexy!

Oh, yes, she looked sexy...

And nobody, but *nobody*, who saw her in this outfit would ever mistake her for a child.

Excitement thrilled through her. Ellie Jasmine knew exactly what she was doing—the woman was a genius. With a sweeping gesture, Briony flung back the curtain, and made the dramatic entrance she knew Ellie was waiting for. Gliding her bare feet across the plush carpet, swaying her slender body sinuously, she moved out into the showroom, feeling like some jungle animal. She could almost hear herself purring... and she could have sworn she heard the rumble of distant drums, as—eyes half closed—she wove her fingers in a deliberately erotic gesture through the silky cloud of blonde hair tumbling to her shoulders——

Oh, dear God!

She blinked and came to an abrupt halt, frozen with her arms still upraised. Ellie was standing by the desk, watching her, clapping her hands in delight... but it was the sight of the figure beyond her—a tall, masculine figure standing outside the shop with one hand already pressed against the plate-glass door to push it open— that had paralysed her.

It was Jake.

And his face was like thunder.

Briony felt her blood turn cold. Oh, lord, she'd kept him waiting, and he had always been a stickler for punctuality. It seemed that nowadays everything she did was destined to upset him.

He was obviously aware that she had seen him, for he swung away and took up a position on the pavement, his back grimly to the door, the set of his shoulders angry and forbidding. Briony stared at him numbly, feeling as if he'd thrown a bucket of iced water over her. Why was she so vulnerable to his disapproval?

Ellie's voice was warm as it broke into her thoughts. 'You look absolutely marvellous. That dress does for you what every dress should do for a woman—it captures the very essence of your personality, and sets a mood.' She moved behind the desk. 'I'll write up a new bill while you're changing. Oh, I'm *so* glad I kept that outfit back. I had a feeling in my bones when I first saw it that it was meant for somebody special.'

CHAPTER FIVE

WHEN Briony joined Jake outside, she didn't feel like somebody special. Seeing the taut, angry expression on his face, she felt like a schoolgirl who had been called to the principal's office for arriving late. And she *was* late, so she apologised—albeit stiffly—as he relieved her of her heavy bag of supplies.

'You see,' she muttered, 'I thought it was just a case of getting the same dress in a bigger size, but they didn't have one, so I had to try on something else...'

Her words trailed away. She had been so taken up with the taut expression on Jake's face that she hadn't noticed the pallor below his tan, a whiteness that hadn't been there earlier. The sight made her heart contract with a sudden indefinable apprehension. 'Jake, are you feeling all right? You're looking——'

'Looking what?' he interrupted harshly. 'Annoyed? Frustrated? What the hell do you expect after you keep me waiting?'

Her concern was swept away by a rush of resentment at his belligerent attitude. 'I didn't keep you waiting that long!' she said defensively. 'Only ten minutes or so.' She pushed her hair from her eyes as a cool gust of wind blew it around her face. At the same time she heard an ominous rumble in the heavens, and felt cold raindrops on her hand. 'Oh, damn,' she said, clutching her Jasmine Boutique carrier and looking around for the Jag but not seeing it, 'there's going to be a thunderplump. Where's the car?'

'There's no parking on this street—I had to park at the other end of Verbena Avenue——'

'But that's *miles* away!' Briony glanced up and uttered a vexed exclamation as she saw the sky was metallic-grey, and a sheet of rain was fast approaching from the direction of the sea. 'We're going to be soaked before we get near it!'

No sooner were the words out of her mouth than lightning shafted across the sky in a blaze of white, and the rain started in earnest. Before she had time to say any more Jake had grabbed her by the elbow with his free hand and had begun manoeuvring her along the street so fast that she had to run to keep up with him.

'Shouldn't we just shelter till it's over?' she cried over the sound of raindrops tap-dancing madly on a canvas awning above their heads. 'We'll be——'

'It's not going to be over... at least, not today, by the looks of it,' he snapped. 'If you hadn't taken so damned long in that shop we would have been in the car before the rain started. If you get soaked it'll be your own fault.' His grip on her elbow tightened and as Briony jerked her head up their eyes clashed, hers protesting, his hard and hostile. 'Surely a little jungle cat isn't afraid of a few drops of rain,' he taunted.

A little jungle cat? What...? Oh... he was referring to her new dress. He had, of course, seen her modelling it for Ellie... and it was quite obvious he didn't think much of it; the curl of his upper lip was evidence of that!

Abruptly, she wrenched her elbow from his grasp. 'Cats don't like their fur to get wet—you know that, surely,' she said, haughtily dashing away the raindrops that were streaming from the tip of her nose.

Ignoring her comment, he just kept striding along, his lips clamped tightly together. And his hands... she sensed that if he weren't carrying her package right now he would have them clamped savagely around her neck!

By the time they reached the car, they were both drenched. As Jake unlocked her door, Briony had to slide past him to get into the passenger seat, and as she did she noticed that his saturated shirt was clinging to his body, the fine white fabric now almost translucent, revealing the dark shadow of the hair covering his muscular chest. Involuntarily, she shivered. There was something very intimate, very disturbing about the sight...

Jake obviously noticed the little ripple of response, but just as obviously misinterpreted it.

'You're cold,' he said sharply. He dumped her supplies in the trunk before joining her in the car and starting the engine. 'I'll put the heater on full blast and that should keep you warm till we get home. Then you can have a hot shower. No point in risking getting a chill.'

Briony slipped her dripping package on to the floor by her feet. Yes, she decided, she would have a hot shower. The last thing she needed was to be confined to bed with a chill. She had so much to do...

A sideways glance at Jake assured her that there was no point in talking with him now about bringing tourists to her studio... not in the mood he was in. She'd do it later—after dinner that evening would be a good time. He'd surely have got over his irritation with her by then.

But, even if he was in a more mellow mood, would he be receptive to her idea? Perhaps in other circumstances he just might, but surely when he realised she planned to use her earnings to pay for her art trip abroad he would refuse her permission outright.

She stared at the hypnotically swishing windscreen-wipers. Devil's Crag did, of course, belong to him, and as owner of the estate he was absolutely entitled to refuse to let her use the studio for commercial purposes.

And he had never made any secret of the fact that what he valued most of all about the Crag was the peace and the privacy he had always been able to count on there.

She had always understood that. Had, in fact, always done everything in her power to help him achieve it.

But what she, Briony, valued most of all was her career... and Jake had obdurately refused to co-operate with her in her attempts to further it.

He was blind, selfish, arrogant—and, of course, autocratic. He wanted to bend her to his will. Well, she wouldn't be bent.

It would be easier, of course, if he allowed her to use the studio, but if he didn't she was just going to have to come up with an alternative plan.

She moved her feet irritably, and as she did knocked over her carrier bag. Bending to set it straight, she noticed a silk headscarf on the floor, half under the seat. Automatically, she picked it up. Jake, absorbed in his driving, paid no attention as she flicked out the luxurious silk square with its terracotta, turquoise and gold medallion design. She traced a fingertip over the exclusive designer label, and as she did the faintest hint of some expensive perfume drifted to her nostrils, a perfume with a musky, mossy base.

So Jake's appointment that morning had been with a woman. And one who could afford to enjoy the finer things of life, if the scarf and perfume were anything to go by!

'Your friend dropped this.' Briony tossed the scarf on to the seat between herself and Jake, and as he glanced down at it briefly she saw his features tighten. 'Does Diane know you're seeing a redhead on the side?'

It was a stab in the dark, but it obviously hit its mark. Jake darted a sharp look at her before returning his attention to the road. 'A redhead,' he said, strain tightening his voice. 'How do you know I was with...a redhead? You...saw us?'

Tension snapped in the air. Oh, not the same tension that had existed a few minutes ago, Briony acknowledged—that had been a hostile tension, the animosity between them hard as steel. A different kind of tension. As if he was waiting, in suspense, for her reply. Was he afraid she'd mention the scarf to Diane?

'No,' she sighed, 'I didn't see you. I just guessed she was a redhead—because of the scarf's autumn colours.' For a second, she considered asking him who the woman was, but when she noticed the almost haunted look flitting over his face she stopped short. What on earth was wrong? Why did it seem so important to him to know whether or not she'd seen him with the woman? It just didn't make sense.

Unless he was afraid she'd find out his friend's identity. Was it possible that she was... *married*?

A sharp pain gripped her heart, but steadfastly she ignored it. If Jake was doing something stupid that was his problem. It had nothing to do with her.

Staring with unseeing eyes through the rain-washed window, she waited impatiently for their journey to be over.

After her shower, she was walking back along the corridor from the bathroom, her hair blow-dried, her body cosily wrapped in her blue robe, when she almost bumped into Jake as he came out of his bedroom. He had changed into a dry sports shirt and jeans, and the casual dishevelment of his still damp hair lent him a look of vulnerability that tugged sharply at Briony's heartstrings. Taken aback at the unexpected acceleration of her pulse, she somehow lost her grip on her hairdrier, and it dropped with a dull thump to the carpet at her feet.

With a nervous, 'Drat!' she bent to retrieve it, but Jake had bent down too. She heard a crack as their heads collided, and dizzily she straightened, wincing as she put a hand to her brow.

'Are you all right?'

She became aware that he was looking down at her with a concerned frown.

'Oh, I'm fine.' Pain shafted through her skull but she somehow managed a light, 'You sure have a hard head, though!'

'*I* have a hard head?' There was a hint of laughter in his voice—the first she'd heard that day. 'I'd say you were the one with the hard head—I've walked into lamp-posts that were more resilient!'

'I don't think there's anything to be gained by arguing about whose fault it was.' For a moment his image seemed faintly blurred, but she noticed he was holding her hairdrier out to her and she took it. 'Thanks. If you weren't such a perfect gentleman, of course, it wouldn't have happened. You'd have let me pick it up myself.'

'I guess there's something to be said for the feminist movement after all.'

In her bare feet Briony suddenly felt overpowered by Jake's size. She'd never really noticed before just how tall he was, nor how tautly muscled was his chest. He smelled of Imperial Leather soap, the clean fragrance overlaid by the musky scent from his skin and hair—a scent that had always been familiar, but one which to her was now tantalisingly erotic. It scattered all her sane and reasoned thoughts... and intensified her senses. Out of the blue she was assailed by an almost overpowering urge to put her arms around his waist and nestle into him; to brush her lips against his throat, and press her nostrils to his skin in an attempt to absorb and inhale the very essence of him.

'That's a nice shirt. Is it new?' The words came sputtering from her mouth in a high-pitched babble. She didn't know which part of her brain had formed them, but it had obviously become aware of her brazen yearning, and wanted to save her from embarrassing herself—and Jake.

'Shirt?' Jake glanced down at the garment in question and muttered vaguely, 'This shirt? No... it's not new. Diane gave me it last Christmas. I——'

'Oh.' Briony's heart contracted as if someone had poked it with a pointed stick. 'Yes, I remember now...'

Her voice trailed away dully. Why was it that she kept forgetting about Diane? She never had in the past; for as long as she could remember she had thought of them as a pair... Jake and Diane. The only thing missing, she had sometimes mused, was an engagement ring on the attractive brunette's long, elegant finger! But now there was someone else on the scene—an intriguingly mysterious redhead.

She had never before had any reason to think of Jake as a womaniser, but then she'd been away at college for the last five years, and knew nothing about his private life during that time. Before that, of course, she had never even thought about such things. Jake could have had ten women dangling at the end of ten strings, and she would have been blind to it. But she wasn't blind now...

'Excuse me, Jake,' she said in a voice she barely recognised, 'I want to get dressed.'

He stepped aside mechanically, and she made to walk by him. She was careful not to touch him, but just being close to him was having an incredibly odd effect on her. Her heart began to bump against her ribs, her legs became wobbly, and her breasts tightened as surely and as shockingly as if he'd brushed them with his fingertips.

'*Are* you all right?' Jake's voice had a harsh edge. 'You look dizzy.'

Briony wanted to draw her eyes from his dark gaze but couldn't. The moment crystallised, and as his concerned words echoed in her ears she realised that she did indeed feel dizzy. More than dizzy, actually: faint, and a little sick.

She placed a hand against the wall to support herself, noting distantly that everything around her was fading into a grey dimness. The blue and dusty rose Wilton runner, the Sanderson curtains hanging at the window in the landing, the chandelier winking at the head of the staircase... all merged into a dream-like backdrop.

And then, as she tried to clutch on to reality and keep her legs from sinking under her, she saw Jake reaching out, heard his voice spiralling between them. It was abrasive, and urgent, and seemed to come from very far away.

'For God's sake, Bri,' he commanded fiercely, 'don't pass out on me!'

She didn't, thank heaven, actually pass out!

But as Jake swept her up in his arms and carried her to her room, and the spinning sensation gradually eased from her head, she had to admit it had been a close thing. She felt as shaky as a new-born colt.

'I'm all right,' she protested as he pulled aside the covers and laid her on the bed. 'I really am.'

'You don't look all right.' His lips were grimly set. 'You look as white as that sheet. I'm going to call Dr Trent——'

'No!' Briony pushed herself up on her elbows. 'I'm all right. It was just a momentary thing. I felt a little faint because I haven't eaten today—I just had a cup of coffee for breakfast. I should go down and make myself some lunch and——'

'You'll do no such thing. Unless you promise to rest a while, I *shall* phone Trent. Polly's right—you've been working too hard, and now it's caught up with you——'

'I'm fine, Jake.' Briony tried to sound convincing, but as pain shafted through her head again she fell weakly back against the pillows.

'*I'll* make your lunch,' he said. 'And if you move from this bed before I come back I'll tie you to the bedposts and turn the key in the lock. Do I make myself clear?'

Briony hissed a two-syllable insult under her breath.

'What was that?' Already half turned to go to the door, he paused, quirking a disbelieving eyebrow in her direction.

'Nothing,' she retorted sulkily.

'I'm relieved to hear it.' A derisive smile twisted his mouth. 'I'd hate to think you had even a nodding acquaintance with the expression I *thought* I heard!'

As he strode arrogantly across the large room, against her will Briony found her gaze drawn to his lean, rugged frame. Until this week she had seen him through a thin veil—a veil of innocence. But now that veil was gone, and she was disturbingly conscious of him as a man. A rugged, compellingly virile man. Rawly, flagrantly male. A man who exuded sensuality, vitality, energy, from every pore of his beautiful body. With a light shiver, Briony allowed her glance to slide from the wide back down to the taut buttocks encased so snugly in his faded jeans... and her breath caught with a soundless gasp in her throat as once again desire blasted through her with the power of white lightning.

She didn't hear his steps disappear along the hallway, because by that time her face was buried in her pillow. Her cheeks were on fire, her blood churned in a hot river through her veins, as she forced herself to face the truth about her passionate reaction to Jake. It was purely physical. It was crude and fierce and shattering. Lust of the most basic kind, lust with a power to consume her, lust with the same potential for disaster as some dread disease.

Oh, how shameful that she should lust after Jake— Jake who had been her guardian, her protector... Jake whom she'd always considered her dearest friend. He would be horrified if he knew how carnal her feelings for him had become.

Despairingly, she curled her slender figure up into a ball and squeezed her eyes shut. For the past few days she'd been irritated and impatient with Jake because he couldn't see that she had grown up, couldn't see that she was no longer the child she'd once been.

Now, for the first time in years, she wished with all her heart that she were that child again.

Jake brought her a white wicker tray bearing one of Polly's willow-pattern bowls filled to the brim with steaming soup, and a matching plate with two buttered wholewheat rolls.

Briony sat up against her pillows and took the tray from him. 'This is ridiculous—I'm feeling fine now. As soon as I've finished eating, I'm going to get up. I have things to do in my studio and I want to get started.'

Jake frowned. 'Things to do?' he asked, thrusting an impatient hand through his hair. 'What things?'

Briony hesitated. She had meant to wait till after dinner to tell Jake of her plans... but perhaps the time to do it was right now? She scrutinised him warily, and saw that his hands were thrust casually into the hip pockets of his jeans, and his eyes were curious.

She made up her mind.

Lifting her spoon, she dipped it into the chicken soup and, sipping a mouthful, swallowed before saying, 'I'm going to do some paintings of the local scenery—I have oodles of old sketches I can work from—and when I have enough to put on a display I'd like to stick up a sign at the end of the lane, inviting tourists to come to the studio and look at my work. And, I hope, buy it.'

It was no surprise to her that Jake saw immediately to the heart of the matter. Even before she'd finished speaking he'd stiffened, and taken his hands from his pockets. 'You're still determined to go on this trip!' His face darkened. 'And despite my opposition you're asking me to co-operate with you.'

Briony's spoon clattered against the porcelain bowl as it slid from her fingers. 'Yes, I am asking... though I don't for one minute expect you to make things easy.'

'Make things easy? For God's sake, Bri, I told you in no uncertain terms that I don't want you to go on this trip!' The words ricocheted angrily around the room. 'I'm thinking only of what's best for you. Can't you trust me?'

'Trust you?' Briony's voice was toneless. 'I've always trusted you, Jake. But this isn't about trust—it's about me being old enough to make my own decisions. Don't worry, I didn't really expect you to agree—I know you hate having strangers on the estate—but I really believe that in other circumstances, if I'd asked your permission to invite tourists to the studio, you'd have said, "Go ahead."'

For a long, long moment he just stared down at her. And as he did Briony felt a twinge of alarm as the colour drained slowly from his face, leaving it almost ashen. She dug her teeth into her lip and was about to say something—anything—to break the painfully taut silence between them, when Jake said, in a voice so low that she could barely make out his words, 'Go ahead.'

His response was so unexpected that Briony's breath seemed to freeze in her throat. Go ahead? Had she heard him aright? Why in heaven's name had he given his permission, when it could only help her achieve an end to which he was diametrically opposed?

'Go ahead?' The words came out in a husky whisper. She felt her shoulders slump helplessly under her robe. 'I don't understand—I thought you'd——'

His gaze was steady. 'Thought I'd what, Bri? Thought I'd maliciously try to stand in your way? No, I'd never do that. Though my father left me the Crag, it is and always will be your home too. Yes, I value the peace and quiet it affords me, but it's a large estate, and I don't think it'll kill me if a few tourists come along the lane to buy your paintings—and if it threatens to, in the evenings or at weekends, Diane and I will take off in the boat——'

Diane and I...

Briony forced her fingers not to tremble as she picked up the soup spoon again. She should have been pleased that Jake hadn't thwarted her plan to use the studio in the way she wanted to; and, indeed, for just a few seconds she had been. And she had felt the old warmth creep around her heart as Jake had murmured that the Crag would always be as much her home as his. Dear, generous Jake.

But the moment he'd said, 'Diane and I'—pairing the two of them as casually, as inevitably as most people would pair Adam and Eve—the bubble of excitement within her had burst, leaving her feeling empty and not quite knowing why.

He turned to leave, but just before he did she caught a glimpse of his eyes, and shock jolted through her when she saw how bleak they were.

Had *she* somehow caused the unhappiness lurking there?

As he pulled the door closed behind him, she called impulsively, 'Jake!'

But the click of the door cut off her cry, and with a soft, 'Damn!' she sank back against her pillows. Just as well, she thought, grimacing. If he'd heard her, and come back, she wouldn't have known what to say.

Thunder pealed across the grey sky and the grandfather clock chimed two as Briony tiptoed down the stairs a while later.

The door of Jake's study was closed. Had he gone out? she wondered. She could hear no sounds of movement, but of course they would be muffled by the clamour of the storm. She knew that her own steps wouldn't be heard, and was glad that she could slip away to the sanctuary of her studio unnoticed. The last thing she wanted—or needed!—right now was for Jake to tell her to get back to bed.

As she reached the foot of the stairs, the extension phone on the mahogany table close by startled her with a sudden shrill demand. She halted, one hand on the newel post. Jake had a phone in his study, and on the days he worked at home most calls were for him. But was he in there? After the third ring, Briony decided he wasn't. She moved quickly across to the table and lifted the receiver, but as she opened her mouth to speak she realised that Jake was in after all, and he had beaten her to it.

His caller was the woman who had phoned him after lunch yesterday. As Briony assimilated the fact, before she could draw the receiver from her ear, she heard the tantalisingly familiar, husky voice say in a tone of some urgency, 'So I can't make dinner tonight after all, but I need to talk with——'

Gently, Briony placed the phone back on its cradle. She hadn't meant to eavesdrop, and she wished she hadn't heard what she had.

How many women did Jake have in his life? she wondered as she moved across to the hall cupboard. There was Diane, and there was this husky-voiced stranger, and there was the redhead with the musky perfume... and, for all she knew, there might be many more.

She took her long red raincape from its hanger and held it absently against her chest as her thoughts spun away into speculation. Did all these women find Jake as attractive as she did? Did they all lust after him? Did they find themselves thinking about him when they went to bed at——?

With an irritated exclamation, she flung the cape around her shoulders. Why on earth was she wasting time thinking about Jake's women? They really didn't interest her in the slightest!

Tugging on her hood, she was just tucking her hair inside it when she heard the door of Jake's study open. A soft, 'Drat!' escaped her lips. Now she was going to have to listen to another lecture! But, no matter what he said, he couldn't force her to go back upstairs again. She was no longer going to let him run her life.

'I have to go out.' His voice sounded right behind her.

Tilting her head round, she saw him take his black leather jacket from the hanger and ease his wide shoulders into it.

'You do?' She forced a casual indifference into her tone.

'I have to meet... someone.'

'Oh.' Briony managed a vague, uninterested tone. 'Who?'

His eyes were dark as they locked with hers. Dark and veiled. She saw a flicker of hesitation cross his features, and then saw his lips tighten. He ignored her question. 'Where are *you* going?' he asked tersely.

'To my studio.'

She had expected an argument, but he just gave a grim nod. 'You're looking better—but take it easy.' One hand already on the front door-handle, he added, 'If you don't feel up to cooking, when I come home I'll take you out for dinner. I'll be back around five.'

'Second fiddle, Jake?' The words were out before she had even realised they had formed in her head. She saw him pause, his eyes blank.

'What the hell's that supposed to mean?'

Her smile was scornful. 'I picked up the phone just now and happened to overhear your lady friend cancelling out. But why settle for dull old me? Give Diane a call and see if she's free... and if she can't oblige I'm sure your fancy little redhead in Falmouth will be only too delighted to cater to your needs.'

There, that should put him in his place! Triumphantly, Briony bent down and rummaged in the cupboard for her rubber boots. She had just tugged on the second one when she was grabbed viciously by the shoulders and yanked upright again. Jake whirled her round so that she was facing him, the menacing glitter in his eyes evidence of his wrath.

'What in God's name has got into you, you little——?'

Briony wrenched herself free. 'What's got into you, you mean!' She glared up at him, enraged that even in the midst of her fury her senses reeled from the incredible beauty of the dark blue eyes slashing into hers. 'Just leave me alone, Jake,' she cried vehemently, 'and stop manhandling me! Who gave you the right to push me around all the time? It seems as if you can't even communicate any more without grabbing me! Why don't you just *go*——?'

'Oh, I'm going!' he grated out savagely. 'I'm going, and don't make dinner for me. I intend to spend my evening in much more congenial company than you can offer!'

Briony ran past him, and, pulling open the door, hurried down the steps, rain battering against her face, wind whirling the hem of her cape around her.

What a storm...

But it was nothing to the storm that was raging in her heart, she thought tearfully as she opened the door of her studio and let the wind sweep her inside. With a choked exclamation, she took off her cape and, shaking the rain from it, hung it on a hook behind the door. For a long time, she just stood there, staring blindly at the rain dripping down on to the plank floor, and letting her misery overwhelm her.

Then, taking in a deep breath, she squared her shoulders, snapped on the light to dispel the gloominess, and crossed to the oak bench where she had earlier left the bag containing her supplies. Work, she decided stubbornly, would block out the distressing thoughts clashing against each other in her mind.

She hoped work would also act as a tranquilliser to soothe the tempestuous confusion in her heart, but at the same time she knew with a woman's deep instinct that that raging storm would not be so easily assuaged.

She spent the afternoon in her studio, and was not displeased with her progress. She timed herself and found that it took her just over an hour to paint one small seascape.

Propping three completed canvases against the window, she scrutinised them, trying to assess them honestly. A sigh escaped her parted lips. Professor Sharp would utter a series of pungent oaths if he saw her slapdash work...

But it was because of him she was doing it!

She turned away, frowning as she figured out how much she should charge for each painting, and just how many she would have to sell to come up with enough cash for her trip. If she worked like the devil, she could finish perhaps eight a day, so that in a week's time she'd be ready to put up her sign at the end of the lane. She was still frowning as she threw on her cape. The professor would swear if he saw her work, but his contempt would be mild compared to Jake's.

The difference was that she cared about Professor Sharp's opinion of her, while she was beyond caring about Jake's! Still, she didn't want him to see what she was doing...

Normally she didn't lock her studio, but today, after only a brief hesitation, she did just that. Then, pocketing the key, she bent her head under the driving rain, and ran helter-skelter back to the house.

She was in bed when, at ten-thirty, she heard Jake come home. She knew that if she hadn't been alone in the house he might have stayed out later, but she also knew that with Poll away he wouldn't want to leave her alone late at night.

No matter how angry he was with her, no matter how much he despised her, he would still protect her. She knew that. And, though the knowledge should have made her happy, it didn't.

And when she heard him turn the large front door key in the lock, heard the lock snap into place, she buried her head in her pillow. The sound, to her, was symbolic; he might as well have been locking the door of the cage in which he seemed so determined to keep her.

CHAPTER SIX

THE following week passed in a blur.

Each morning Jake left for the office before Briony got up, and she spent every minute of the day painting, breaking only to make dinner for the two of them. She served his in the kitchen, but took her own to the studio, where she ate abstractedly while getting on with her project.

If this arrangement displeased Jake, he made no mention of it. How different it was, she reflected bitterly, from those previous, precious times when Polly had left them on their own, and they had gone sailing or hiking together in the evenings.

But by the end of the week she had more than achieved her goal of eight canvases a day, and late in the evening of the seventh day, just before sunset, she walked along the half-mile winding lane to the highway, and, with excitement churning her stomach, she nailed her newly painted sign to a weathered post at the side of the road. She was just giving the nail one last firm swipe with her hammer when she heard a car pull in on the shoulder right behind her. Shading her eyes from the rays of the dying sun, she squinted at the unfamiliar green sedan that was parking a dozen feet away.

The passenger door opened, and a familiar figure hopped out, a smile on her face, a small suitcase in her hand.

'Polly!' Briony rushed forward to welcome Jake's aunt with an energetic hug. 'What a lovely surprise! But why didn't you let us know you were coming home tonight?'

'It was a spur-of-the-moment decision, dear—I got a drive from one of Ron's friends who was coming this way.'

A voice hailed them from the car. 'Cheerio, Poll!'

Polly waved. 'Thanks again, Lorne...'

As the car zoomed away with its headlights on, Briony asked, 'How's Kate?'

'Just fine...and the baby's already gaining weight nicely. Ron has found a lovely Scottish nanny—she arrived today. And, though I love the wee ones, I'm glad to be home. I'd forgotten just how exhausting small children can be!

'But you've obviously been busy too!' She scrutinised Briony's brightly painted sign. '"Local artist—local scenes. Landscapes, seascapes for sale. Studio hours ten till eight." That's a long day, dear! Your sign's very attractive, though. It'll draw people in, I'm sure. So...' she quirked a questioning eyebrow '...Jake didn't mind?'

Briony hoped Polly wouldn't notice the colour rising to her cheeks. 'Here, give me your case—I'll carry it.'

Together they began walking along the winding lane towards the house, a slight breeze brushing the long grasses on either side. 'No,' Briony said, 'Jake was very fair about it. He said the Crag was as much my home as his, and he'd just keep out of the way if the tourists bothered him.'

'Where is he?' Polly glanced up idly as a buzzard soared in the darkening sky with a mewing cry.

'He took Diane out for dinner.'

'Ah...'

Briony thought that was all Polly was going to say, but after a long moment the older woman said quietly, 'Such an unlikely pair, but time and circumstances have formed a bond between those two that I doubt anything could break. A bond that was forged after Jake's mother—my sister Emma—died.'

'Jake was fifteen then, wasn't he?'

'Mm, almost sixteen. No longer a boy, yet not quite a man. And he wanted so much to react like a man to his mother's death—or rather to react as he *thought* a man should react, as his father did: gruffly, unemotionally. But Jake was far more sensitive than his father, and not yet able to cope with his grief in such a disciplined way. I was living up north at the time, looking after my invalid mother, but Jacob—my brother-in-law—would phone me often, for he was worried sick about Jake. The boy wandered the moors alone all that summer, keeping everything bottled up inside himself. Wouldn't talk to anyone...'

Briony had heard the story before. Many times. But she had always listened to Polly as if hearing it for the first time. 'Go on, Poll,' she murmured.

'And then the Denhams moved to the Folly. Apparently Diane was out riding her horse one day, and she stopped to talk to Jake...and when she discovered he was a neighbour she asked him home for dinner. The lord alone could tell us what moved him to accept her invitation.' Polly shook her head, a soft smile on her face. 'Anyway, that was the turning-point. You know what a motherly soul Prue is; she took the lost young lad into her heart. And before long Charles took an interest in him too, encouraged him to take up golf. Even got him a membership at the club, and introduced him to some other boys his own age who were keen on the sport. Within a year, Jake was, to all intents and purposes, his old self again. But he never forgets a good turn, and I believe that he'll always have a soft spot for Diane——'

'Is he in love with her, Poll?' Briony heard a roughness in her own voice.

Polly paused to pluck a dog-rose from the hedge beyond the verge. Holding the pink-petalled blossom to her nostrils, she inhaled the delicate scent a moment, before tucking the flower into the buttonhole of her blouse. 'Jake and I were talking,' she said finally, 'the day after you came home—and from what he was saying I think wedding bells are in the air at last.'

'Really?' Briony stumbled, as if Polly's words had been a trap hidden on the path. 'What...exactly...did he say?'

'He said he was going to do something he should have done long ago. And I said, "You mean, Diane and you?" And he said, "Yes, Poll, that's it." What else could that mean but...a wedding?'

Briony's grip tightened on the handle of the case. 'It certainly sounds that way, doesn't it?' It could also mean, she thought, that he was planning to tell Diane that there was someone else in his life, but there was no point in saying that to Polly. It would be pure speculation.

'Yes, dear. And isn't that exciting...for the two of them?' Polly walked for a minute or so without saying any more, and then she went on quietly, 'But of course that means I shall have to find a new home.'

Briony stopped and stared at her. 'Find a new home? Why on earth would you——?'

Polly stopped too, and looked up at her wistfully. 'Stands to reason, doesn't it? Once Diane becomes mistress of the Crag, there'll be no room for me.'

Again the buzzard's cat-like mew wailed across the sky above them. This time, to Briony's ears, it sounded like a cry of unhappiness. 'How strange,' she murmured. 'I've never actually pictured Jake married...it's just that things have stayed this way so long. Don't you hate change, Poll? I detest it. I suppose I'll have to look for a new base too.'

'Oh, no, dear,' Polly protested. 'It's different for you. I'm just the housekeeper and almost ready to retire anyway...though I was glad of the job when Jake offered it me after your poor ma died—but *you* won't have to move out!'

Briony shook her head. 'I couldn't stay on at the Crag...I just couldn't. It would be...' Unbearable. She couldn't say that to Polly. She wouldn't understand. But it would be unbearable to lie in her bed each night, knowing that Jake and his wife were in another room, close by, making love... 'It would be so much nicer for the newlyweds to have the house to themselves.'

They rounded the corner and as the turreted building came into view, its granite glowing a beautiful golden-pink in the evening sun, Briony felt tears blurring her eyes.

The Crag. How she loved it. Had loved it since the first moment she'd set eyes on it, fifteen years ago. She loved the house, loved the endless pounding of the surf on the jagged black cliffs below, loved the bleak, familiar face of the moor and all the creatures that lived on it.

It was going to tear her apart to leave.

And, with things the way they were now between herself and Jake, once she left she doubted she'd ever come back.

'I'll take this one—*Cornish Sunrise*—and I think...' The young Canadian woman pushed her sunglasses on top of her head as she swithered between Briony's painting of *Trelawney's Woman* anchored in the bay, and a dark depiction of the moor with storm clouds threatening. 'The moor. It makes me think of Heathcliff, honey.' She smiled up at her husband who was peeling notes from a bulging wallet.

Briony wrapped the two canvases carefully, and, handing over the package, walked to the door of the studio with the couple as they left. As their car disappeared round the corner, she looked at her watch. Almost seven-thirty. They would, she was sure, be her last customers for the night. Her sign had been up for almost two weeks now, and she had already learned that by early evening most travellers were no longer interested in shopping; what they were interested in was getting to their hotel, or finding a B and B before it got too late.

Time to call it a night.

Stretching her arms above her head wearily, she turned back into the studio. Automatically setting straight some of the canvases propped up along the bench, she emptied the coffee carafe into the sink, and rinsed it out. Only then did she move to the makeshift till. Opening the drawer, she withdrew the money she'd made that day, feeling the same surge of surprise and pleasure she'd felt each night when she'd seen the amount of crumpled bills stuffed there. But before she could count them she heard a sound behind her. Startled, she clutched the notes against her chest, and wheeled round to see Jake leaning idly against the door-jamb, watching her. The sun was at his back, and it cast a golden sheen on top of his dark head.

'"The queen was in her counting house——"' his voice was low, and softly mocking '"—counting all her money..."'

'Very funny, Jake.' Irritated, Briony tightened her lips and shoved the wad of notes into the pocket of her jeans without looking at them. 'What do you want?'

He pushed himself from the door and walked forward, his eyes never leaving hers. 'I thought it was time I came to see what was so...valuable that it had to be locked up.' His gaze glittered challengingly.

So he had discovered that she'd started locking her studio. When had that happened? And had he guessed it was to keep him from seeing her work? 'How do you know I——?'

'Because I happened to pass your studio early this morning, and I was curious to see a sample of the pictures all these tourists have been carting away with them.'

Still he hadn't looked away from her, still he hadn't so much as glanced at the canvases stacked on every surface in the studio. 'So you tried the door and found——'

'Found I couldn't get in.'

Briony wished he hadn't come; she didn't want him to see her work. The pleasure that had flowed through her a moment ago drained away. 'Well,' she said coldly, 'you're in now. What are you waiting for?'

'Waiting for your permission to have a look around.'

'My permission?'

'I don't want to look at something you don't want me to see, Briony.'

She felt her face burn as the blood rushed to her cheeks. He knew. How could he not? He was playing with her, as a cat might play with a mouse, teasing it, relishing every suspenseful moment, before pouncing for the kill.

She shrugged, angry with him, but somehow angrier with herself. It had always been that way with the two of them—Jake had a gift for making her look at herself with total honesty, without even saying a word. 'Go ahead,' she muttered. 'But hurry up—I'm just closing for the night.'

'Thank you.'

She leaned back against the sink as, slowly, he removed his gaze from hers. He slid his hands into the pockets of his grey trousers, and began wandering around the studio, looking as elegant and sophisticated, damn him, as if he were browsing in the Louvre. From under her lashes Briony fixed her gaze on his face, searching his expression for the slightest hint as to what he was thinking.

It took him several minutes before he had examined every one of her canvases—including the one on the easel: a painting of *Trelawney's Woman* coming home at sunset. She'd painted it that morning between customers; it was exactly the kind of thing her art school friend Rhona would have scornfully called 'Bright, flashy, trashy'; it was, without doubt, the very worst example among all her items for sale.

It was the last one he looked at, and he stood there, with his back to her, for what seemed to Briony an endless stretch of time.

She braced herself, waiting for the torrent of anger he would shower on her. Anger and contempt. Biting her lip, she watched him turn.

His face was grave. And his eyes were filled not with hostility, as she'd expected, but with a deep sadness.

'I knew you wanted to go on this trip, Briony,' he said quietly. 'Until this moment, I just didn't know how much.'

Taking his hands from his pockets, he walked over to her, looked down at her. Briony felt her mouth go dry as he reached out and smoothed the thick blonde hair back from her brow. 'Little Bri...' his voice was taut '...determined to go her own way. Determined to make her own mistakes.'

She felt perspiration run down her spine, felt it tickle the small of her back. She closed her eyes.

His lips caressed her forehead so lightly that it was like being kissed by a butterfly's wing. She smelled the faintest hint of wine on his breath, and the faintest scent of some spicy shampoo from his hair. The moment seemed to freeze in time, but she couldn't capture it, couldn't hold it. In the space of a heartbeat he was gone, his footsteps echoing in the evening stillness as he crossed the plank floor. She heard the click of the door as he closed it behind him, and only then did she open her eyes.

The fragrance from the pots of lemon-scented verbena and ivy-leaf pelargonium which Polly had arranged on a stand outside, under the open window, drifted into the warm studio on a fluttering breeze. The exquisite summer sweetness of it brought a piercing ache to Briony's heart.

An ache that added to the pain already there. The pain caused by Jake's reaction to her work.

Easier to bear, she thought tormentedly, if he had ranted and raved at her. She could have lived with that; she deserved that.

What she didn't deserve was his kindness. And what she couldn't accept was his disappointment in her.

She brushed the back of her hand over her eyes, and felt the warm salt tears on her skin.

Damn! she gritted out with a savage kick at the sturdy leg of the bench. Damn, damn, damn! Why was she feeling so lost, why was she feeling so confused! It was the teenage years that were supposed to be the years of turmoil, when emotions—hormone-driven—went wild... but she was no longer a teenager. She was a woman of twenty-two, a woman of the times—confident, poised, mature. Why, in her case, had these tumultuous, mixed-up feelings been so long delayed?

She sensed that the answer lay deep inside herself, but it seemed to be veiled by a thick mist, and every time she came close to uncovering it the mist swirled all around it again, as if protecting her from something that she was not yet ready to know.

Next morning a soft, light drizzle blocked out the sun, and turned their little corner of the world into a greywashed watercolour. It was the kind of weather that Briony had always thought lent a strange magic to the air.

But there was no magic in the air today. Only tension. Tension between herself and Jake.

He was silent and withdrawn over breakfast. Polly was planning to nip over to Prue's later to pick up some cuttings, but not even his aunt's happy chattering roused him to any kind of conversation. He got up from the table right after he'd eaten, announcing that because he had a heavy day ahead, and clients to see in the evening, he was going to spend the night in town. It was something he did on very rare occasions, and only when it was unavoidable.

Briony was in her studio when, around nine, she happened to look out of the window and saw a flash of silver in the grey wraiths of mist still lingering over the drive, and knew that it was Jake whizzing away in his Jaguar. Some time later, Polly took off in the Vauxhall, peeping the horn in cheeky farewell before disappearing from view. Briony plugged in the coffee-maker and as her glance fell on the picture on the easel she was reminded of Jake's reaction to it... and at the same time reminded of the way she'd melted when he had brushed the tender kiss over her brow.

Steadily she forced her thoughts to the day ahead. It was going to be a busy one—Bridgeport's annual Old-Tyme Festival Week was due to begin that afternoon and the occasion always brought hordes of tourists. So she, Briony, could surely expect some of those tourists to come trooping to the studio.

She would have time, she decided, to complete at least one painting before they began to arrive. With a bit of luck, she might even manage two!

The sound of a car coming along the lane disturbed her as she was putting the finishing touches to her third canvas, and, to her surprise, when she glanced at her watch she saw that it was almost twelve. Putting down her brush, she walked to the window, and was in time to see Polly's Vauxhall sail along to the front door. The mist had burned away, and the day was now sunny, with just a few clouds drifting across a blue sky.

Turning back to her work, she paused with a frown. She had been so engrossed in what she had been doing, she hadn't noticed that she hadn't had even one customer all morning. Surely her luck wasn't about to break?

Her stomach rumbled aggressively, and she patted it. OK, she muttered to herself, may as well go have some lunch.

Polly had gone inside by the time she reached the house, but just as Briony was about to open the front door Jake's aunt whirled out again, halting briefly as she almost bumped into Briony.

'Oh, there you are, dear—glad to have caught you. Della just phoned—you know, my best friend at the gardening club. She and I have been invited to have a private tour of Lady Beresford's rose garden... very spur-of-the-moment thing, but we've been hoping for ages...

You see, Della and Lady Beresford are very distant cousins about twenty times removed and Lady Beresford has just recently found out about the relationship, and wants to get to know Della! Isn't it exciting? Can you manage to make yourself some lunch?'

'Oh, I think so,' Briony retorted wryly. 'I just hope when I'm your age I have half your energy. See you... when?'

'Probably not till late.' Polly got into her car, and, slamming the door, called out through the open window, 'Lady Beresford not only has the nicest rose garden in the district, she has also a cordon-bleu chef! Della's hoping we'll be asked to stay for lunch... and maybe dinner too!'

After the Vauxhall disappeared, Briony stood staring into space for a long moment. How tempting it would be to jump in her own car, and, like Polly, take off somewhere for the day. Maybe even drive into Bridgeport, for the opening of the Old-Tyme Festival! This would be the first year in ages that she'd missed it.

But she didn't have time. She had made quite a bit of money the last couple of weeks, but she still needed a lot more. And she had only a week left.

Blowing out a sigh, instead of going up the steps to the house, she started walking back to the studio. If she went into the house to make lunch, she just might miss a potential customer. She couldn't afford to do that.

And she wasn't really very hungry anyway.

She stayed at the studio till dusk, existing on cups of coffee, and as she walked back to the house she decided wearily that it had been the longest day of her life.

Not one customer. Not one, all day. She just couldn't believe it. It was as if someone had put a curse on the place!

And the frustrating thing was that when she'd stood at the door of her studio, and held her breath and listened, she could hear the cars humming along the highway. A steady hum. A steady hum that continued all afternoon long. But for some reason not one vehicle left the main road to come down the lane; not one of the many tourists on the road came to buy her paintings.

Was it because of the festival? Had she misjudged what the tourists would do? Were they going straight to Bridgeport, not wanting to stop on the way?

Whatever the reason, she hadn't made a single penny. That would certainly please Jake if he knew, she thought with a scowl...

She had just closed the front door behind her, when she heard the sound of a vehicle outside. Polly...

She opened the door again, and poked her head out into the twilight... to see not the Vauxhall, but a light grey van—one she didn't recognise—pulling up at the foot of the steps. The driver was leaning out of the window. Yelling.

'Hey, kiddo—it's me!'

'Tony!' Shoving the door wide open, Briony ran down the steps, getting to the van as her friend jumped down on to the gravel. 'How super to see you!'

And it *was* super, she thought as he whirled her round and planted a kiss on her lips... not garlic tonight, she noted wryly, but olives. Clutching her arms around his neck, she returned his affectionate kiss energetically, and then looked up at him, her eyes sparkling. 'You couldn't have come at a better time. I'm all on my own, and I was beginning to feel sorry for myself. Are——?'

She hadn't heard a second vehicle come along the lane, so when the snarl of car tyres on the gravel reached her ears it snapped her words off, and a moment later she and Tony were trapped in the spotlight as a powerful vehicle braked to an abrupt halt alongside the grey van.

Blinking against the strong white beams, Briony peered beneath the curve of her hand to ascertain the identity of the new arrival. But as the headlights faded away all she could make out was a tall male figure emerging from the car and slamming the door vehemently.

'It's your guard dog,' Tony murmured, laughter in his voice. 'Uh-oh, watch out—here he comes...'

Jake? Briony stared disbelievingly. He was supposed to be in Bridgeport!

Though her first, instinctive reaction was to wrench herself free of Tony's embrace, she conquered it. She knew how it would look to Jake, seeing them in this clinch, but she also knew how it would look if she and Tony were to break furtively apart—as if they'd been caught doing something they were ashamed of. Heart hammering furiously, she watched Jake approach.

'I didn't think you were coming home tonight——' she began tentatively, only to be interrupted rudely.

'That's quite obvious!' Even if Jake's tone hadn't been icy the contemptuous curl of his upper lip would have left Briony in no doubt as to his mood.

'What on earth are you implying?' Briony retorted in an outraged tone.

'What do you think I'm implying? When the cat's away...you know the rest! You didn't expect me home tonight...and you knew that Polly had been invited with her friend Della to stay over at Lady Beresford's, so you decided to have a little——'

'Now just you back up, Jake!' Indignantly, Briony glared at him. 'I did *not* know that Polly was staying over at Lady Beresford's——'

'She left a message with my secretary saying she wouldn't be home tonight...and she said she'd be phoning to let you know too.'

'She might have tried to call me,' Briony said frostily, 'but since I've been in the studio since she left here I wouldn't know.' What a *boor* the man was, she fumed—how could she ever have thought him charming?

She felt Tony's fingers run playfully up and down her spine. 'Good evening, Mr Trelawney,' he murmured. 'Pleasure to meet you again.' Though his tone was polite, Briony could hear the bubble of fun just below the surface. 'I decided to take Bri up on her offer to camp here—do hope you don't mind.'

Oh, but Jake *did* mind—very much! Briony could tell by the wave of anger coming from him.

'I'm going to lock up in a few minutes.' Jake marched past them up the steps, not letting his eyes once alight on Tony. 'So you'd better show your friend where to go and get back inside, Briony.'

Any anger he was feeling paled beside the anger he had stimulated inside *her*! 'You don't have to worry about me, Jake,' she said with exaggerated sweetness, 'I have my own key. Tony and I have so much...catching up...to do—I think I'll join him in his tent for a while.'

Jake didn't answer. He didn't even turn round. Briony heard his footsteps crash across the hall, recognised the sound of his study door open, heard it reverberate as he slammed it shut. And despite the warmth of Tony's body next to hers, and the comfort of his arm around her waist, she felt cold. As if the door Jake had slammed shut weren't the door to his study, but the door through which he himself could be reached. And he'd shut her out of his life.

She stayed in Tony's tent till close to three in the morning, and with the help of a few glasses of the white wine he'd conjured up to go with the salted nuts and pretzels she'd brought to the tent he had coaxed her into a lighter, happier mood than she'd been in for days.

Not till her eyelids became so heavy that she could scarcely keep them open did she decide she'd better get back to the house before she fell asleep where she sat. 'Oh, lord,' she giggled as she tried to get to her feet, 'I'm a bit tipsy. It's time I was in bed.'

'I can't persuade you to share my sleeping-bag?' Tony already knew what her answer would be; it was evident in his self-mocking tone. 'OK, I can guess what you're going to say: "We're friends, Tony, don't spoil it."'

'Sorry, Tone!' Briony finally managed to scramble up and, yawning widely, she pushed aside the flap opening of the tent. As she straightened and stepped outside, the night air hit her face with the quick stealth of an unexpected slap. 'Lord but it's cold out here... and dark! I can't see a thing.'

Tony's body suddenly loomed up beside her. 'It *is* dark! Let me see you to the door.'

'Oh, no, thanks, Tony... I know my way blindfold. See you in the morning. Let's forget about that swim, though! Come to the back door when you get up and we'll have breakfast together.'

The grass was wet and it made the soles of Briony's trainers slippy as she ran. She hadn't felt cold in the tent, but now she felt herself shiver. She saw the shape of the house up ahead, but it was very vague. No lights were showing. Jake had probably been in bed for hours, she reflected sourly—though how he could sleep she didn't know, with so much hostility and anger seething inside him!

Lost in her thoughts, she tripped on the bottom step at the front door. She was just lurching upwards again, a soft oath on her lips, when a cold, familiar voice slashed through the dark.

'So you finally decided to call it a night... or rather, a morning!'

'Jake!' Briony peered up into the dark, seeing only a shadowy shape and a glitter where his eyes would be. 'What a fright you gave me—I didn't see you!'

'Have you been *drinking*?'

She realised that her breath must be reeking of wine; there was no point in pretending it wasn't. And why should she? It was just that his voice, which had been icy before, was now cold enough to freeze blood—even blood liberally laced with alcohol, as hers was! She couldn't see him, but she was intensely aware of his presence a few inches away as she swayed light-headedly in the pitch dark. Surprisingly, instead of feeling intimidated, she felt extremely dignified as she answered with a regal tilt of her head, 'Yes, I've had a glass or two of wine with Tony.'

The words, which she had enunciated so carefully, sounded as if she'd blown them through cotton wool, but though their edges were fuzzy they were perfectly clear to her... and obviously clear enough to Jake also.

'A glass or two!'

The tone of his voice conjured up a vivid picture in Briony's mind. She could imagine his hands clenched into fists, she could almost see the grim set of his jaw, hear the perfect white teeth grinding together like the grinding of mortar and pestle.

A giggle started somewhere in her diaphragm and gurgled out like the sound of water being sucked down a sink. 'Please excuse me, Jake.' She felt so dignified that she could almost feel a tiara crowning her head. 'It's getting chilly. I'm going to bed.'

She reached out to where she expected the door-handle to be, but instead of encountering a knob found her fingers hitting a solid wall of muscle. Jake's chest? His stomach?

While she was trying to decide which, and trying to orientate herself, she somehow—she didn't understand how—found herself leaning against the wooden door, her back pressed against the studded panels. Jake wasn't touching her, but she knew she was trapped. She could sense him standing facing her, and sensed that his forearms were on either side of her head, his palms face down against the door. He had caged her.

As he always did!

'Jake, I'm really tired—I want to go in.'

He wasn't touching her. He didn't have to. His male aura had reached out to her senses, entangling her more potently than the cage he had made with his arms. The night air infiltrated her senses, the heavy scent from the rose-beds mingling with the disturbing scents from Jake's body. It was an aphrodisiac of the most powerful kind, seeking out a response from the most primal part of her being.

'Not till you tell me what's going on between you and that——'

'It's absolutely none of your business what's going on, Jake! I'm twenty-two, I don't have to answer to you or——'

'What the *hell* were you doing down there till this hour?' Jake's voice had a thick, congested quality that set Briony's nerves tingling with almost painful excitement. It was the same unfamiliar tone he'd used on the beach, when he'd caught a glimpse of her half naked.

'Probably the same kind of things you and Diane and all your other women do when you're alone together,' she retorted. 'Oh, we probably don't do them with quite the same skill,' she went on mockingly, 'since we haven't been at it for as long as you have, but——'

His hands were on her shoulders now, suddenly, angrily. The fingers dug into her flesh, making her wince. He shook her, hard, and her teeth chattered. Her head, already spinning from the wine, began to feel like a whirling top. Resentment swelled inside her, giving her the strength to wrench herself free from his grip. Ducking under his arms, she made for the door and scrabbled wildly for the handle. She couldn't find it, and a frustrated sob was gathering in her throat, when she felt her legs begin to give way under her. Felt herself begin to slide down the door.

Jake must have had better night vision than she did, for he caught her, and pulled her to her feet. She heard him swear as she slumped against him, and as she threatened to slide down again he pulled her against him. His arms were like steel around her, his thick-knit wool sweater scratched her cheek, his breath, sweetly familiar, riffled over the top of her head.

She was wearing thin cotton shorts and a T-shirt, and she could feel his rock-hard muscled outline pressing against her. It was exquisite agony. Her head dropped back, her lips parted. Every cell in her body was vibrant, expectant. She felt her breasts swell eagerly, felt the nipples tauten as the blood surged to the sensitive peaks. Was it the effect of the wine? It must be... she'd never felt like this way before, so wanton, so meltingly——

'Get inside!' His harsh voice ripped into her silken musings, tearing them apart so abruptly that she jumped. He wrenched the door open, and as it creaked on its ancient hinges he took her by the shoulders in a grip that was far from gentle, and almost threw her into the hallway. Stumbling to catch her balance, Briony felt a sob gather in her throat. This was like some nightmare—it had to be a nightmare, a nightmare from which she was going to waken any minute!

But it was no nightmare. As the door crashed shut, light flooded the entryway, and she saw Jake standing there, just inside the door, fists planted on his hips, eyes burning with a strange, wild fire.

'Get upstairs,' he blazed. 'And don't even think of sneaking out again tonight. If you try, I'll go down there and kick that ape off my property so fast, he'll wonder what hit him.' With one lean hand, he dragged his black hair back from his brow. 'And I'll make sure he never wants to come back.'

Misery. Sheer, utter misery. Briony had never before experienced the agonising, aching misery she was feeling now. What had happened to Jake? What had caused this heartbreaking change in him? He was turning her whole world upside-down, a world that had for the longest time been so safe, so beautiful, so... so perfect.

'Oh, Jake...' The sobs that had been gathering in her chest rose painfully in her throat, but she managed to choke them back, managed to choke back the cry of despair. She looked at him, blinking furiously to fight the tears that threatened to well in her eyes, digging her teeth savagely into her lower lip in an effort to stop its trembling. Hugging her arms around her shaking body, she turned from him and stumbled to the stairs.

As she moved like a robot up to the landing, feeling as if her legs were going to give out at any moment, she knew, without looking back, that Jake hadn't moved. Knew he was standing like a statue. Frozen. Watching her.

Watching her the way a guard would watch a prisoner. A prisoner in a cage. A prisoner he didn't trust.

CHAPTER SEVEN

'I'LL have a nice hot breakfast ready for you in a jiffy.' Briony laid half a dozen rashers of bacon on a grooved dish and popped it in the microwave. 'Here——' she pushed a mug of coffee across the kitchen table to Tony '—have some of this while you're waiting. I'll just get you some butter and marmalade for your toast. Or would you prefer something else? There should be some of Polly's homemade raspberry jam here. Would you like that? It's really delicious. Or perhaps I could rustle up some honey. Which——?'

'Briony!' Tony's voice cut her off in mid-stream and she turned towards him, startled by the firm, commanding tone he'd used.

'Yes?'

'For God's sake, slow down! You've been prattling like a feather-brain ever since you opened the door to me! What the devil's wrong?'

'Wrong? What do you mean?'

'Am I the problem?'

'Tony,' she protested, 'there *is* no problem.'

'You never could tell a decent lie, could you? So it *is* me. I thought as much. Last night, after you left the tent——'

'Yes?' Briony felt her cheeks grow warm. How did Tony know anything had happened after she left him? 'What about... after I left your tent?'

Tony pushed back his chair and stood up. 'I wanted to make sure you'd got in safely, so I followed you for a little way, then waited—waited to hear the door open...'

Briony uttered a vexed exclamation but Tony continued, 'What I did hear was Jake tearing you off a strip for being with me. God, I felt awful. I almost thundered up there and confronted him; but I guessed you'd rather I didn't. Why in God's name do you put up with that tyrant? I hate like hell to see you so unhappy.'

Turning her back so that he couldn't see the tears misting her eyes, Briony slid two slices of bread into the toaster. 'He's not really a tyrant. I told you last night—it's just that he still thinks of me as a child.'

Tony took her shoulders and gently turned her to face him. Lowering his head, he laid his brow against hers. 'I want you to be happy, Bri. You mean a lot to me.' His arms tightened round her in a comforting embrace.

'Oh, Tony, you mean a lot to me too...'

Her words, almost inaudible in their quiet intensity, were interrupted by the sound of the microwave beeping. Automatically glancing round, Briony felt her heart tremble as she saw Jake standing in the open doorway.

He was dressed in a dark grey business suit, with a white shirt and silver-grey tie with a discreet purple motif. His hair was brushed back and his jaw had a freshly shaved look. Despite his sophisticated appearance—or perhaps because of it—he seemed to Briony to be the very essence of everything that was male. His appearance was elegant, but the elegance was a veneer—a veneer that only emphasised the rugged, sensual man beneath. He was all the way across the room from where she stood, yet even at twelve feet his raw masculinity snaked towards her like a lasso, capturing her within its deadly, imprisoning coil.

'Jake...' She shivered, and felt Tony's arm tighten protectively around her. Unable to help herself, she leaned back against him. How long had Jake been standing there? How much had he heard?

'I thought you'd have gone by now,' she said weakly.

'I've decided not to go in today. I'm going to work here, in my study.'

Tension crackled between them. She knew only too well why he was staying home—and *he* knew that *she* knew! If he went to Bridgeport, she would be alone here with Tony...

Before she could come up with some snappy response, she heard a sharp knock on the outside kitchen door. She was closest to the door, and she turned to open it. Diane was standing on the patio, a smile on her red-painted lips, the sun gleaming on her brown hair. She looked like a *Tatler* fashion-plate, Briony thought, in her tailored white shirt, grey jodhpurs, and richly polished high leather boots.

'Good morning, Bri. Hi there, Jake.' She walked past Briony into the kitchen, halting abruptly as she saw Tony. Obviously taken aback, she stared at him and Briony bit back a smile as she saw that Diane, whose friends were either very rich, or titled, or both, was clearly unimpressed by Tony. 'Oh, sorry,' she said, with a little sniff, 'I didn't realise...'

'That's all right, Di.' Briony stifled a nervous giggle as Tony rolled his eyes in her direction. 'This is Tony Price, a friend of mine—Tony, I'd like you to meet Diane Denham, our neighbour.'

'Oh, the camper.' Diane's tone was dismissive. 'I saw the tent when I drove up just now.' She held out a limp hand to Tony and winced perceptibly as he crushed it in his great paw. As soon as he released her, she turned her back on him pointedly and addressed Briony. 'I came over to ask if you'd like to come to Bridgeport with me, for the day.'

'I'm afraid I can't; I'm going to be working in my studio. Didn't you notice my sign at the end of the lane?'

'Sign?'

'I'm selling my paintings. I posted a huge sign just at the turn-off——'

'Oh, I didn't notice,' Diane said vaguely. 'But you know me—I always look straight ahead when I'm driving. I'd pass my own mother if she were hitch-hiking on the highway! So...you can't come. That's too bad.' She drummed her fingernails impatiently on the counter-top. 'I wanted you to come to the festival with me—it's the horse show today.'

'Sorry, Di...'

'Darling?' Diane tilted her head provocatively towards Jake. 'You couldn't, I suppose...?'

Jake shook his head grimly. 'I've brought work home.'

Tony chuckled. 'God, I used to love horse shows—haven't been to one in years, though. I used to make my pocket money as a kid by helping a groom at one of the local stables, and in July and August he'd take me to the shows with him. They were the highlights of my summer.'

Diane flicked long fingers through her gleaming hair and when she spoke it was as if she hadn't heard one word Tony had said. 'Well,' she sighed, 'I've wasted my time coming over, haven't I? Patsy's abroad, and Mavis Duff is up north, and the Tremartin twins can't come because their parents have guests from London staying with them. I certainly shan't go on my own. It's no fun at all.'

'There's no need to go on your own,' Tony drawled lazily. 'I'll take you to the horse show, love...if you don't mind my old van.'

Diane's features stiffened. 'Oh, I wouldn't dream of asking you to——'

'No problem.' Tony pinned Diane with a mocking look, and Briony could just feel the challenge quivering in the air between them. It was quite plain that Tony could read Diane like a book and just as plain that he didn't like what he was finding between the pages. Was he hoping to take her down a peg or two? 'If you'll just hang on,' he said levelly, 'till I get some sustenance, we can hit the road.'

Diane moved her slender shoulders restlessly. 'Oh, it's not going to kill me if I miss it——'

'Look——' there was a steely glint in Tony's eyes '—what's the problem? You want to go to the show, and you want someone to go with. I've offered to be your escort. All you have to do is wait for ten minutes——'

'Far too kind of you.' Diane smiled, and Briony saw the faintest hint of smugness in her eyes. 'But I really don't want to hang around. I'm anxious to be on my way. Why don't you have your breakfast, and I'll go on ahead, you can follow in your...van...when you're ready? Perhaps we can meet up there?' She turned swiftly and made for the patio door. 'I'll call you tonight, Jake. Bye, Briony——'

'You won't have to hang around,' Tony said smoothly. 'If you're in such a tearing hurry, I'm sure Briony won't mind if I don't join her for breakfast.'

Diane's face was suffused with pink, the thwarted expression in her eyes revealing her frustration. Tony chuckled, a mischievous sound, and then, turning his attention to Briony, drew her into his arms.

'Sorry about breakfast, kiddo. Hope you have a good day at the studio.' And then, to her huge astonishment, he kissed her. Not his usual casually affectionate kiss, but a thorough, passionate kiss that left her speechless. As he let her go, he threw her a surreptitious wink, and she realised he'd kissed her like that to upset Jake.

And he *had* upset Jake.

When the door leading to the patio had clicked shut behind Tony and Diane, she sneaked a look at his face, and it was a dull, angry red.

'Well, they've gone for the day.' She turned her back on him as she took the toast from the toaster and inserted it into a silver toast-rack. 'No need for you to have stayed home,' she went on quietly. 'I can't get up to much mischief on my own, can I?'

There was no answer, and when she turned round she found she was alone. Beyond the gently swinging door, she heard his footsteps fade away along the hall.

Perhaps he'd decided to go in to the office after all, she decided wearily. But when she passed his study a few moments later she heard him inside, talking on the phone.

Her heart felt heavy as she went out the front door and closed it softly behind her. How she hated fighting with him. Yes, she was still angry with him for refusing to let her have the money for the trip. That was one thing. But to be constantly bickering with him, sparring, needling each other—that was something else. Something totally alien to her nature... and, she knew, something totally alien to his.

She was going to go on the trip, and he must realise by now how serious she was about it. So why couldn't they put the quarrel behind them, and try to put things back on a friendly footing?

Someone had to make the first move... and she was going to be the one. She'd make lunch and set it out on the patio, and she'd invite Jake to join her. She knew he would accept. He had never been one to hold a grudge.

The morning, from a business point of view, turned out—unexpectedly and devastatingly—to be exactly the same as the morning before. Not one customer materialised to buy, or even look at, her work.

Briony stood in the doorway of her studio at twenty to twelve, listening to the distant hum of traffic from the highway. It was steady, and carried easily to her ears in the quiet of the summer day.

She looked along the lane, her eyes following the track till the curve closed it from her view. What was wrong? she wondered frustratedly. Was everyone in such a hurry to get to the festival that they didn't want to stop? Was her sign too plain? Perhaps it needed something to dress it up.

She hauled out a long scarlet streamer from one of the cupboards. It was nylon, and would stand up to any vagaries of the weather. Even Diane would surely have noticed her sign if it had been festooned with the wide gaudy ribbon.

Feeling better now that she was doing something positive, Briony ran lightly down the lane towards the highway, trailing the streamer behind her. Why hadn't she thought of it before? she wondered as she got to the end of the lane. Why hadn't she——?

She stopped abruptly, feeling as if someone had punched her in the stomach as she stared at the post on which she'd nailed the sign a couple of weeks before. The post itself was still standing there, weathered and stout... but the sign had disappeared. And, apart from the deep hole in the wood where she'd driven the large nail, there was nothing to show it had ever been there at all.

Where had it gone?

A thorough search in the brambled hedges and nettle clumps along the highway, and among the foxgloves at the head of the lane, gave up no clues as to the whereabouts of the board. Ignoring the traffic whizzing by, Briony leaned back against the post and stared up at the cloudless blue sky. No wonder she'd had no customers, she thought bleakly.

Who would have done such a thing?

Trailing the streamer disconsolately behind her, she made her way back along the lane. She'd lost a day and a half. It would take her an hour or so to make another sign and nail it up again. Her plans to have lunch with Jake would have to be shelved. She was too pressed for time.

His study door was still closed as she crossed the front hall, and her trainers made little sound on the slate floor as she passed it and walked to Jake's little workshop at the back of the house. Among other things, he kept his golf clubs there, and his fishing tackle; it was a room she rarely had cause to enter, but this was where she'd found the board she'd used for her original sign. At the time she'd noticed a couple of other boards of a similar size, and with a bit of luck they'd still be there.

Flicking on the light, she looked around the windowless room, and relaxed as she saw that the boards were still there. In fact, one was exactly the size she needed—the same size as the one that had disappeared from the post.

Turning it over, Briony stared, at first disbelieving what her own eyes were telling her. It was her sign. Oh, the wood was cracked roughly where someone had banged it from the post... but it was her sign, all right. 'Local artist—local scenes. Landscapes, seascapes for sale. Studio hours ten till eight.'

Horror prickled over the surface of her skin as the full implication of what she was seeing sank in. Jake. *Jake* was the one who had smashed the sign down.

Briony sank back against the door-jamb, eyes tightly closed. Dear God, how mistaken she had been about the kind of man he was. Never in a million years would she have believed him capable of such a despicable, underhand action.

For long moments she stood there, her mind spiralling despairingly downwards as she tried to come to terms with this new situation. When, finally, she did, she lifted up the sign determinedly, along with a hammer and a couple of large nails, and made her way out of the workshop again.

She would put the sign back. And she would let Jake know she'd found out about his wretched little manoeuvre.

But not now. Not when she was so upset. She didn't want him to realise how much it had hurt her to find out that he wasn't the scrupulously ethical person she had always believed him to be; she didn't want him to know that he had the power to wound her.

Later, when she had gained some sort of control of her emotions, she would tell him... in terms that would let him know exactly what she thought of him... that she had found out what a snake he was.

* * *

'Aren't you stopping for lunch?'

Briony jerked her head towards the door of the studio as she heard Jake's voice. 'Lunch?' She managed to make her voice indifferent. 'No, I'm not very hungry.'

He was still wearing his dark grey trousers, but he'd discarded his jacket, and he'd pulled his silk tie loose at his throat. 'Polly phoned. She won't be home till late. She suggested I take you out for dinner.'

Out for dinner...with a snake? With an effort, Briony managed to bite back the words. 'Thanks for the offer, Jake, but I can't leave the studio till after eight.' She levelled a hard glance at him. 'My sign...you know? The one at the end of the lane—people will expect me to be here till then.'

If she'd been expecting to see a guilty reaction, she was disappointed. His eyelids didn't even flicker. 'Busy, are you?'

'I didn't have any customers yesterday, nor this morning,' she said evenly, 'but I expect things are going to pick up again now.'

'Why's that?'

She took a deep breath. 'Someone stole my sign, but I found it and nailed it back to the post again. I know who did it, Jake——'

'Stole your sign?' Jake frowned. 'Who the devil——?'

Whatever Jake had been going to say was drowned out by the sound of voices outside. Briony hadn't heard a car, but as she glanced through the window she saw a battered old Range Rover parked at the head of the lane, and a plump, bespectacled woman coming up the path to the studio. She was accompanied by a teenage girl with frizzy brown hair.

Jake moved back to let the couple enter the studio, and Briony slid her hands into the pockets of her jeans as the woman smiled and began to walk slowly along by the bench, examining the pictures.

'Over here, Grandma!' The girl's eyes sparkled. 'This one would be perfect for Mum, for the front bedroom.'

The pair stood side by side, and in the silence Briony found herself looking at Jake. He was looking at her, his eyes enigmatic. For no reason Briony felt her cheeks turn warm, and she was about to turn away when she heard the woman say, in a voice that was quiet but carried to her ears, 'No, darling—these are very disappointing. We've wasted our time stopping. Let's get along now— perhaps we'll have more luck when we get to Falmouth.'

Briony felt as if she'd had a bucket of cold water poured over her. The woman wasn't wearing ultra-fashionable or expensive clothes, but she certainly looked as if she could afford to buy any of the canvases set out on the benches, and Briony had hoped to make at least one sale. Instead, the stranger had dismissed her work out of hand. Intensely aware that Jake was watching her, Briony tried to keep her emotions from showing on her face. The last thing she wanted was for Jake to know how the criticism—justifiable or not—had hurt her.

Tensely, she waited for the pair to leave, but as the woman walked towards the door she stopped with a frown, her attention caught by the sketches thumb-tacked to the whitewashed wall.

'What is it, Grandma?' The teenager's voice was bright and questioning. 'Do you like those?'

'Very much.' The woman's mouth curved in a smile as she stepped forward a little so that she could examine the sketches more closely. 'Very much indeed. They're absolutely delightful.' The sound of a bird singing outside trilled into the silence as she continued to scrutinise Briony's finely detailed work. 'Absolutely delightful.'

'Are these for sale?'

The teenager's blunt question made Briony blink. She turned, and found that the question hadn't been directed at her, but at Jake. Both women were looking at him.

A lazy smile twisted his features, and Briony saw the teenager blush. 'You'll have to ask the artist...' He gestured in Briony's direction.

Briony stepped forward. 'I'm sorry,' she said in a quiet voice. 'They're not for sale. I've done them over the years... just for my own pleasure...'

'This is all your work?' The older woman sounded astonished. 'The canvases...and these fine drawings are done by the same person? You could knock me over with a feather—oh, I do beg your pardon! How very rude of me...please forgive me. It's just that...'

Briony knew exactly what she meant. And all of a sudden she felt so ashamed of the rough canvases, and filled with a sort of remorse that she'd disappointed this stranger, that she said impulsively, 'The sketches aren't for sale, but I'd like to give you one. Whichever one you'd like to have.'

Eyes that were an unusual turquoise colour fixed on Briony for a long moment, as if the owner was trying to look right inside Briony. Then she smiled, as if she liked what she saw. 'How very kind of you. I *should* like one, dear. The bee is precious, but I think...' she tilted her head to the side as she ran her gaze again over all the sketches '...I think my favourite is the barn-owl. You've given him *such* a personality, with his lap-top computer and bleary eyes...'

Briony rolled up the picture and secured it with a rubber band before handing it to the stranger. 'There,' she smiled, 'I hope you enjoy it.'

'Thank you so much...' The turquoise eyes held a hint of apology. 'I don't even know your name!'

'Briony. Briony Campbell.'

'Briony—how pretty. I shan't forget it. And the address of this studio——'

'Oh. Devil's Crag, near Whitstable Tor.' Why on earth would she want to know the address? Briony wondered.

'Devil's Crag.' The stranger repeated it thoughtfully, as if trying to memorise it. 'Thank you again, dear. Now come along, Megan, your mother will be waiting.'

For a moment Briony had almost forgotten about Jake's presence. But as the cheerfully chattering voices of the tourists faded away outside he said softly, 'Why didn't you charge her for the sketch, Briony?'

Snake, she thought, as she turned a scathing glance in his direction. 'You know damned well why I didn't, Jake. Now if you don't mind I have work to do.'

'What were you saying earlier, about your sign having been stolen?'

The man had nerve, there was no doubt about it! But if he thought he could goad her into revealing how he had upset her, he was going to be disappointed. 'Oh, nothing,' she said airily. 'Some jerk removed it from the post but I found it and put it back.'

'You said you knew who did it?'

How could he look so innocent... and how could he look so heartbreakingly attractive? Angry with herself for the way she melted when she looked at him, Briony ignored the little voice in her head that tried to remind her of how she had intended to play this scene. Contemptuously, she said, 'Oh, let's stop playing games, Jake. You stole my sign, you'd stoop to anything to get your own way——'

'What the hell are you talking about?' Jake stepped forward, his eyes blazing. 'I never touched your bloody sign. Oh, I saw it! And yes, I wanted to rip it down—but I didn't. I told you, Briony, I'm going to have to let you make your own mistakes, since you seem determined to do so.'

'I never thought I'd ever say this to you, Jake, but... you're a liar! You——'

She felt a surge of apprehension as she saw the furious glitter in his eyes. 'What did you call me?' he demanded, his voice harsh with disbelief.

Her legs began to tremble. Pressing back against the edge of the bench to steady herself, she drew on all her courage. 'A liar, Jake. That's what I called you.'

For a moment she thought he was going to hit her. Never, in the fifteen years since she'd known him, had she seen him so angry. His face was a dull crimson, a vein bulged frighteningly at his temple, and his eyes...

His eyes were the eyes of a stranger.

Briony felt as if an icy hand had clenched itself round her heart. Her breath seemed to be frozen in her throat; it was almost impossible to get air into her lungs.

'I think we should forget about dinner tonight.' The revulsion in his tone was like a dagger in her heart. 'In fact, I think you and I should keep out of each other's way as much as possible from now on.'

The rigidity of his shoulders as he strode across the studio showed clearly how angry he was. And, storming out, he slammed the heavy door savagely shut behind him.

As the sound reverberated in Briony's ears, she sank down on to a stool, the events of the last moments draining every last bit of strength from her body. She'd really done it this time. The relationship between herself and Jake was now finally, irrevocably damaged beyond repair.

And as she put her head in her hands and let the tears run down her cheeks she had to admit the shameful truth. Even though she knew he was a liar, and even though she despised him for the rotten trick he'd played on her, she was still deeply, helplessly attracted to him.

CHAPTER EIGHT

'WELL, finally!' Briony ran down the front steps to meet Tony's van as she saw it sweep round the corner from the lane around eight o'clock next morning. She rested her fists lightly on her hips as he pulled the vehicle to a halt and jumped out. 'Where on *earth* have you been? I went along to your tent an hour ago and when I found it empty——'

'Sorry, love, if you were worried—Diane invited me to stay the night at the Folly, and it was too late to call and let you know.' Wryly, Tony rubbed the back of a fist over his stubbled jaw. 'As you can see, I haven't shaved yet.'

Briony stared at him disbelievingly. 'Diane invited you to stay over? But...why? It was quite obvious yesterday that the two of you didn't exactly hit it off!'

Tony put an arm around Briony's shoulders. 'Kiddo, I'm not even going to try to understand what happened. I've never met a more exasperating woman in my life. Every time she opened her mouth, and came out with yet another snobbish remark, I felt like choking it back down her throat. But yesterday...' he shook his head bewilderedly '...yesterday was something else. Despite the sparks that flew between us all the time, it was the most fun I've had in years.'

'And last night?' Briony couldn't help the mocking note in her voice. 'Was that fun too?'

A warm finger was pressed against her lips for a brief moment. 'Ask no questions, my pretty.'

'And are you...going to be seeing her again?'

Tony's frown was almost imperceptible. Had Briony not known him so well, she might not have noticed it, or the flicker of regret in his green eyes. 'It would seem not,' he murmured lightly. 'I'm just a struggling artist without a job, and Diane...' He shrugged. 'The beautiful Diane made it quite clear this morning that starving in a garret is definitely not her scene.'

'But if the two of you hit it off so well——'

'Chalk and cheese, my love,' Tony said. 'Chalk and cheese. And now,' he added with a quick, dismissive smile, 'I'm going to be on my way. You have your work cut out for you if you're going to make the money you need for your trip, and I don't want to be a nuisance. Oh, and talking of your trip——' he grimaced '—you'll never guess who was at the horse show.'

'Who?'

'Angelique St Clair. I didn't know she came from Cornwall.'

'Yes, she lives in Falmouth, with her grandmother. Did you speak to her?'

'Mm. And I wish I hadn't! I opened my mouth and stuck my foot right in it. I happened to mention in passing that I'd bumped into you... and I told her that Sharp had invited you to join him on his tour. Dammit, I'd completely forgotten you said he'd invited her originally and she'd had to turn down the opportunity because she couldn't come up with the money.'

'Oh, Tony...' Briony's voice was edged with dismay.

'Her face crumpled up and her eyes became sort of haunted. God, I could have just kicked myself. Anyway, she mumbled some sort of excuse and slipped away.' He frowned. 'I ran after her to see if she was all right, and apologise if necessary, but before I could catch up with her she'd got into her car, and she shot past me without even seeing me. She was crying.'

'Oh, Tony, you must have felt so awful——'

'She was driving a top-of-the-line Mercedes, Bri.' Tony's green eyes were puzzled. 'That really threw me. If she can afford that kind of car, how come she couldn't come up with the money for the trip?'

Briony shrugged helplessly. 'I've no idea, Tony... but that's what Professor Sharp told me. Anyway, you didn't mean to upset her, so try to forget all about it. Would you like to come in for a coffee... and a shave,' she added with a chuckle, 'before you go?'

'Thanks for the invitation, Bri, but I want to get on my way before the roads start to clog up with traffic.'

It didn't take long for Tony to take down his tent, and after giving Briony a boisterous, affectionate hug, and a promise to drop her a note once in a while, he piled all his things into the van and took off again down the lane.

Briony stood watching from the foot of the steps. How uncharacteristic it had been of Diane to invite Tony to stay over. But if she'd been so taken with him, why had she given him the brush-off this morning? Had she merely been using him? Had she begun to suspect that she wasn't the only woman in Jake's life, and decided that the way to bring him to heel was to make him jealous? *Would* he be jealous if——?

'Your friend, I see, has gone.'

Briony swivelled round as she heard the sardonic voice behind her. She had left the front door ajar when she'd come out, and hadn't heard Jake cross the hall. He was dressed for the office, and was immaculate in a beautifully cut navy suit. Arrogant, superior, mocking. All those words applied to him, Briony thought as she looked up at him. And not to forget sneaky, she added, as she recalled the rotten trick he'd played on her the day before. Well, she decided bleakly, she wasn't above being nasty too!

'Yes, he's gone...' she threw him a taunting smile '... but I shouldn't be surprised if he turns up again one of these days. He and Diane hit it off rather well yesterday and Di invited him to spend the night at the Folly.'

Other than a slight narrowing of Jake's eyes, his expression gave nothing away. 'And how do you feel about that?' he asked in a smooth voice.

A WOMAN'S LOVE

'Never mind about me.' Briony thrust a hand irritably through her hair. No one else had the power to get under her skin the way this man had been doing lately! He brought out the worst in her—made her say things she normally wouldn't have said. 'Rumour has it that the sound of wedding bells is in the air for you and Diane—how do *you* feel, knowing your intended bride spent last night with an ape, as you once referred to Tony?'

Jake's lips tightened. 'You've turned into a vicious little thing, haven't you? And you should never listen to rumours, Briony. Diane and I are good friends, nothing more.'

So Polly had been wrong—Jake hadn't planned on proposing to Diane. But what *had* he planned on telling her, then? That he was in love with someone else? Had he already told Diane? Had she invited Tony to stay over just to show Jake that he wasn't the only fish in the sea?

'If not Diane, then... for whom are the wedding bells going to toll?' Briony stared up at him with an insolent gaze that she hoped would mask her emotional turmoil. 'Do tell me something about the woman of your choice, Jake!'

A muscle twitched in his jaw, and for a moment Briony thought that he wasn't going to respond. Then, abruptly, he said, 'The woman of my choice?' A gull screamed overhead, but Briony didn't take her gaze from his, and as she looked at him she saw his eyes take on a distant expression, almost as if, involuntarily, he had drifted away into a private dream. 'She's young,' he murmured slowly, 'and she's innocent. And the woman of my choice is very beautiful——'

At his words, Briony felt a leaden plunging of her heart. She herself fitted the first part of his description—though Jake, of course, would have no way of knowing just how innocent she was; she had never lacked for dates with the male students at Marwyck, but, despite thinking herself half in love once or twice, she had never been sure enough of her feelings to go that final step. But as for the rest... Oh, she knew she wasn't plain, but she would never, ever have described herself as 'beautiful'.

'A secret love, Jake?' An inexplicable pain lent a jeering quality to her question.

He blinked, and stared at her, as if he'd forgotten for that fraction of time that she was standing there—and regretted speaking his thoughts aloud. His eyes lost their far-away look and became hard and unreadable.

'That's right, Briony.' His tone was mocking. 'A secret love.' He frowned, and glanced impatiently at his watch as if he was all of a sudden bored with the conversation. 'Now, if you'll excuse me, I have more important things to do than stand around exchanging unpleasantries.'

Unable to come up with a sarcastic retort, Briony hugged her arms around herself as he strode away towards the Jag with long, purposeful strides. He didn't look at her as he drove off, not by so much as a glance letting her know that he was aware she was watching him.

She waited till the car disappeared round the bend in the lane, and she might have stayed there for much longer, the heaviness of her thoughts weighing her down, had she not suddenly heard the telephone ringing in the front hall.

She ran back inside and, lifting the receiver, said in a slightly breathless voice, 'The Crag—Briony speaking.'

'Bri, this is Diane. Look, Daddy wants to take us all to the club tonight—to the dinner-dance. I know Polly won't come but we'd love it if you and Jake would join us.'

Briony grimaced. The very last thing she wanted to do was spend an evening in Jake's company. And though he hadn't referred this morning to her harsh accusation of the day before she had felt his hostility bristling under the surface all the time they'd been talking, and had he not said last night that from now on the best thing would be to keep out of each other's way as much as possible?

'That's awfully kind of you, Diane, but could I take a rain-check? I'm afraid I'll be down at the studio till eight...' Her tone conveyed regret very eloquently, Briony decided, with no hint that the regret wasn't genuine.

But her satisfaction was short-lived. 'No problem! You know we never eat till around nine-thirty when we go to the club. And Bri, you must wear your new jungle-print dress. Ellie told me about it—I can't wait to see it——'

'Diane, I don't know that Jake will want to go out this evening. I don't even know if he has other plans——'

'Leave Jake to me,' Diane said firmly. 'Put him on the line.'

Briony had to admire Diane's attitude. If Jake really had jilted her, she was acting as if nothing had changed in their relationship. How she wished she herself could be so cool where he was concerned! 'Jake's gone to the office.'

'Then I shall get in touch with him there. Now I must go. If you don't hear back from me by noon, then you'll know everything's all set, and we'll see you there.'

Briony blew out a frustrated sigh as she heard Diane hang up. She had always found it difficult to assert herself where Diane was concerned, and this time had been no exception.

But Jake never did anything he didn't want to do.

And she knew that he didn't want to spend time in her company.

So Diane would be phoning back. Probably within the hour. She would catch Jake with her invitation as soon as he reached the office.

And his response would be a resounding refusal.

'You're jumping around like a hen on a hot girdle! What on earth ails you, dear?'

Briony had been pacing the kitchen, a mug of coffee in one hand, the last morsel of a freshly baked scone in the other. Now she paused, and turned to look at Polly, who was getting up from the table.

'I've been waiting for Diane to phone back to say Jake isn't able to go to the club tonight,' she replied. 'And——'

'But you told me Diane was going to call before noon if plans were cancelled. It's well after twelve now, dear.' Polly opened the dishwasher door and slid in her empty plate and mug. 'So it seems as if the dinner party's on.' She looked around the kitchen vaguely. 'Now where did I put that special can of spray Lady Beresford's gardener gave me for my roses...? Oh, there it is. Now...are you going back to the studio, dear?'

'Mm.' Briony glanced at her watch. 'Oh, I must dash. You'll be out on the patio? You'll hear the phone?'

'Don't worry, I'll hear it... if it rings.'

It didn't.

And Jake didn't come home till seven, when he went straight into the house after parking the Jag by the door.

Watching him from the studio, Briony caught a fleeting glimpse of his face as he went up the steps, and his grimly set expression didn't bode well for the evening ahead. She sighed. Perhaps he'd been in court and had a bad day, perhaps the belligerent thrust of his jaw had nothing to do with the prospect of having to take her to the club.

She had an hour to wait before she found out. After showing out a last, lingering customer, she made her way across the long shadows cast on the lawn by the evening sun. She had crossed the hall and was just about to ascend the stairs when Jake came out of the drawing-room.

'I thought I made it quite clear yesterday,' he snapped without preamble, 'that it would be best if we kept out of each other's way?'

Frowning, Briony stopped and looked up at him. His eyes were dark with anger. 'I don't believe I indicated that would be a problem,' she retorted icily. 'So what's biting *you*?'

'We're going to the club tonight, aren't we?' he demanded.

'Since I haven't heard otherwise from Diane since this morning,' Briony spat back scathingly, 'yes, I suppose we are.' She tossed her hair back in an arrogant gesture. 'Obviously you accepted the Denhams' invitation.'

'*I* accepted the invitation?' Disbelief hardened his tone. 'What the devil did you expect me to do when Diane told me how keen you were to go?'

Even as she heard the barely contained frustration pounding in his words Briony realised what had happened. Her expression of regret, faked though that regret had been, had completely backfired on her. 'Diane called you and said I... wanted to go?' she asked faintly.

'My, you even manage to sound surprised!' Savagely, Jake dragged open the top button of his dress shirt, and with the fingers of one hand slackened his perfectly knotted tie with a fierce flick of his wrist.

Briony felt a quick surge of irritation. 'You can stay at home, then, and I'll make excuses for you. I'll have a much better time anyway if you're not there breathing over my shoulder, finding fault with everything I do——'

Even before he broke in, she knew that, being the gentleman he was, he wouldn't let her go to the club unescorted. 'How long will it take you to get ready?' he said roughly.

'Half an hour.'

With an angry twitch of his powerful shoulders, he swung away, and strode back into the drawing-room.

To her surprise, just as she reached the landing, she heard the ping of crystal against crystal, and guessed he was at the bar, pouring himself a Scotch from the decanter.

She paused for a moment, her hand on the railing. As a rule, Jake didn't drink on his own. Had he lost an important case? Had someone at the office upset him? Or was *she* the one who was causing him to seek the numbing effect of alcohol?

At any rate, she acknowledged as she walked across the landing to her bedroom, he would have no more than one drink. He was a very reasonable individual and he knew he would be driving to the club.

But that wasn't what was concerning her... it was the fact that he felt it necessary to have a drink at all!

'You could have knocked me down with a feather when I saw you walking into the clubhouse in that sexy little leopard-skin number!' Robb Tremartin swung Briony expertly around the dance-floor at the Bridgeport Golf and Country Club, his handsome face creased in a grin. 'Good God, it seems like just yesterday that you and Mel were cycling to school together in your neat little navy and grey uniforms. You always were a pretty kid, of course, but who'd have guessed you'd turn into such a stunner?'

'And who would have guessed you'd turn into such an accomplished flatterer?' Briony smiled up at her partner, but as she did she couldn't help comparing his reaction to her appearance with the way Jake had behaved when she'd come downstairs earlier in the evening.

He and Polly had been in the drawing-room, Jake over at the bar, Polly sitting by the hearth, when she'd walked through the doorway. Polly had noticed her first, and Briony had found herself wishing she had a camera as she saw the expression of stunned disbelief in Polly's eyes. The older woman's gaze was wide as she stared at the carelessly tousled blonde hair tumbling in disarray around Briony's shoulders, and it widened even more as it moved down over the leopard-skin dress that clung with such sleek sensuality to her small but voluptuous figure.

'Bri, dear, is it really you?' Polly put a hand to her heart, and Briony saw her lips tremble. 'Oh, my goodness... Jake...'

From the corner of her eye, Briony saw Jake turn—sensed, rather than saw, him stiffen. She felt her breath catch in her throat. She already knew that he didn't like her outfit. Would he be hypocritical enough to pretend, in front of his aunt, that he did?

'Walk across to the bar, dear——' Polly's voice quivered with excitement '—and spin around so we can admire you.'

'Oh, I don't think so——'

'Do as Polly says, Briony.' Jake's cool tone broke in as she started to protest. And then, softly, for her ears alone, he taunted, 'How about a repeat of the jungle-cat routine?'

Before Briony could respond the phone rang in the hall, and Polly jumped up, saying, 'Oh, I think that's for me. Della said she was going to call. Excuse me, dears.'

The door clicked shut behind her, and Briony felt the tension that always quivered between herself and Jake when they were alone snap tautly into place as if on cue.

'What are you waiting for, Bri?'

Briony looked directly at him, and when she saw him shove his hands arrogantly into his pockets, saw the hard challenge in his gaze, she felt the now-familiar resentment start to simmer inside her. Why was he so *abrasive*? Could he not, for once, be pleasant? Her heartbeats thudded against her breastbone as her anger quickly flashed from simmer to full boil, blotting out the little voice inside her that warned her not to do anything she would regret.

'You want jungle cat, Jake——' she raised her eyebrows and levelled a derisive gaze at him '—*I'll* give you jungle cat!'

It was the dress, she realised afterwards, that made her act the way she did. Ellie had been right; it created a mood. And the mood it created was...provocative, reckless, sultry.

Keeping her gaze fixed on Jake, she ran the tip of her tongue, suggestively, across her upper lip, moistening the red-lipsticked flesh. Then, running her palms in a lazy, seductive way up her thighs, she began walking towards him. She made a soft purring sound in her throat as she caressed the silky fabric clinging to her hips, and, half closing her eyes, she wove her fingers in a deliberately erotic gesture through her long blonde hair, releasing the musky scent she'd sprayed there earlier.

She glided right up to Jake, and just as she reached him she pirouetted. 'Well,' she said coquettishly, 'how was——?'

He caught her by the shoulders, and pulled her so close that her face was just inches from his. 'That's a dangerous game you're playing, Briony.' His voice was thick and harsh.

She tossed back her hair and said breathlessly, 'It's a game you asked me to play, Jake. Now you want to stop... Why? Are you suddenly afraid it's a game you can't win?'

His eyes burned with a dark fire. There was anger there, of course, but there was something else—something almost frightening in its intensity. But before Briony could decipher it she heard the door-handle being turned. With an abrupt twist, she wrenched herself from Jake's grip, but before she could stumble away he had grasped her elbow with a cruel hand and taken control of her again. Ignoring her small cry of protest, he manoeuvred her across the room, and when an apologetic Polly appeared in the doorway he said smoothly, 'I'm afraid we'll have to leave now, Poll...'

'You'll be the belle of the ball, Bri,' Polly called from the front door as they got into the Jag. 'Maybe you'll find yourself a nice young man!'

Robb Tremartin was certainly a nice young man, Briony thought wryly as she brought her mind back to the present, a much nicer man than Jake! Too bad he wasn't her type. He had been at one time, though! At the memory, she found herself chuckling.

'What's so funny?' Robb's voice was curious.

'I was just remembering,' Briony smiled, 'that when I was sixteen I had an agonising crush on you. I had the devil of a job keeping it from your sister! I lived in dread of Mellie finding out and telling you——'

'Had I only known,' Robb said, with a mock groan. 'But listen, it may not be too late for us. I do have a fiancée who's teaching in Wales in a town that has a quite unpronounceable name—our wedding's set for December, as a matter of fact—but I think I could wangle my way out of it...'

'If you can't——' Briony looped her arms around his neck and vamped him shamelessly from under long, fluttering eyelashes '—don't worry. I'll settle for a little love-nest and a large bank account. And darling...' she faked a throaty bedroom whisper '...I'll make it worth your while...'

It was flirtation at its most harmless, and Briony was enjoying it, was just beginning to forget about Jake and the bitterness between them, when she caught sight of him close by, and felt her heart give a jarring shudder.

He was dancing with Diane, his gaze distant, brooding, as if his thoughts were a million miles away. Thinking of his secret love? Briony wondered. And if so, which one? The mysterious redhead? Or the woman with the hesitant, husky voice? As jealousy shafted through her, shocking her with its unexpectedness, Jake blinked, and became aware of her. Their eyes met and locked, and for an electric moment something shafted between them with a force that sucked Briony's breath from her lungs.

Everything in the place seemed to come to a standstill. Everything disappeared from her consciousness except Jake.

Tonight he was wearing a teal-blue sweater over a button-down shirt in a stone colour, and a pair of trousers in a darker shade of stone. The overwhelmingly male impact of him brought a surge of hot colour to Briony's already flushed cheeks. Unexpectedly, she felt her knees sag, and as she involuntarily tightened her grip around Robb's neck it must have looked to Jake as if she were deliberately taunting him. She saw his lips curve in a derisive twist, and even as her heart cried out in protest he whirled Diane round and swept her away, and they were immediately lost to sight in the crowd.

She was barely aware of what she was saying as she continued the light repartee with her partner, didn't even notice when the band stopped playing, till Robb gave her a hug and said warmly, 'Thanks for the dance, Bri.'

'It was fun.' She managed a smile. 'Perhaps we can do it again later on——'

'I should be so lucky,' Robb teased as he dropped a casual kiss on the top of her head. 'You're going to have to beat off all the would-be Tarzans tonight. Now, let me take you back to your table——'

'I'm going to pop by the powder-room first. Thanks again, Robb.'

What was wrong with her? she wondered miserably as the door of the ladies' room swung shut behind her. A moment ago, when she'd met Jake's eyes, she'd become feverishly hot, her cheeks had felt as if they were on fire.

But now she felt as chilled as if she were sinking into an icy cold, bottomless pool.

She stared at herself, at her pale, pinched face in the bright mirror, as she delved deep inside herself in an attempt to come up with an answer. And with a suddenness that made her feel as if the floor were dropping out from under her the swirling mists cleared from her heart, and the truth was revealed in all its frightening splendour.

Stunned, she gazed into the wide grey eyes that looked mockingly back at her.

You're not just physically attracted to Jake, they told her. You're in love with him.

How had it happened? And how could it have happened without her realising it? Something so earth-shattering, so——

'Bri—I was wondering where you'd got to!'

Through a fog of confusion Briony heard the voice at her side. Startled, she blinked, and saw Diane's reflection beside her own, in the mirror.

'Oh...hi, Diane.' Forcing a smile, she turned towards the other woman.

'You're enjoying yourself?' Diane opened her evening bag and extricated her lipstick.

'Yes—dinner was lovely. It's ages since I've had lobster...' Oh, if only this fog of confusion would lift from her mind. She didn't want to talk to Diane...she didn't want to talk to anybody. She wanted to think about Jake...and her newly discovered feelings for him.

Diane smoothed raspberry lipstick over her chiselled lips. 'You...saw Tony this morning, before he left?'

'Mm. For a few minutes. He said...you wouldn't be keeping in touch?'

To Briony's amazement, Diane's brown eyes flickered with a shadow of the same regret that had briefly darkened Tony's eyes that morning.

'That's right,' Diane said quietly. 'We were just...ships passing in the night...'

Her words trailed away, leaving an awkward little silence. Briony broke it by saying, 'Look, you're probably wondering if Jake knows Tony slept at the Folly.' She took in a deep breath. 'He does, Diane. I told him.'

'Oh, I don't care about that.' Diane waved her lipstick in a dismissive gesture, and, putting it back in her bag, turned with a rueful smile. 'Bri, I think it's time I let you into a secret. Jake and I have never been lovers. When I was younger, I must admit there were times when I wished... But it just wasn't on the cards.'

How odd, Briony thought. Had Diane told her this a few weeks ago, she'd have been fascinated to hear about it. Now, she could barely fake an interest in carrying on the conversation. She had something else, much more pressing, to think about. 'But you seem so...close...when you're together,' she murmured, finally.

'It's an act, Bri. Ages ago, Mummy and Daddy started nagging me about getting married and settling down, so to keep them quiet I told them a little white lie—I said Jake and I had an "understanding".' She grimaced. 'They—unfortunately—mentioned it to Jake! He didn't give me away, but later he tore me off a strip! Afterwards, though, he said he'd go along with it—that he didn't *really* mind, because he wasn't involved with anyone. I told him if he ever did fall in love, of course I'd let him off the hook.'

'So you're not in love with Jake...and he's not in love with you.'

'No.' Diane's eyes became thoughtful, and she played absently with the heavy gold chain at her throat. 'But...'

'But...what?'

'We talked, that last night he took me out for dinner, and he told me he wanted to end the little charade. Well, obviously he must finally be in love with *someone*, Bri! But, whoever she is, she's certainly not making him happy! If I knew who she was, and could get my hands on her, I just might strangle her! I don't know what kind of game she's playing, but I've never seen Jake so...so darned miserable as he's been lately. I don't suppose you have any idea who the woman could be?'

'No,' Briony said. 'No, I haven't.' Just go, she urged fiercely, silently, I need to be alone...

'I think I might have seen her.' Diane lowered her voice as someone came into the room. 'In Falmouth one morning. I was crossing Verbena Avenue when he passed in the Jag and I caught a glimpse of a woman in the car with him. Oh, it was just a glimpse, but I could see she had gorgeous red hair and pale skin. Rather delicate-looking—not his type at all, I would have thought. It was a couple of days after you came home—I was still suffering the tail-end of that dreadful migraine...'

That would have been the morning she and Jake went to Falmouth, Briony thought distractedly. And the redhead would have been the woman who had so carelessly dropped her luxurious silk scarf...

'Ah, well——' Diane shrugged '—I just hope she's good enough for him!' Glancing at her watch, she added, 'I'd better be getting back to the table. Coming?'

'In a minute...'

Diane nodded, and, giving herself a last quick appraisal in the mirror, she made for the door.

As it swung shut, Briony slumped back against the wall, the conversation with Diane quickly evaporating from her mind as her thoughts veered relentlessly back to her own unhappy situation.

How could she have been so *stupid*, she agonised, as not to have realised what was happening to her? How could she have been so blind as not to notice when her long-time affection for Jake had begun to evolve into something so devastatingly, frighteningly different?

She was in love with him. And she knew it was the kind of love that lasted a lifetime. She knew there would never be anyone else for her.

And Jake not only despised her... he was, according to Diane, in love with someone else.

How as she going to get through the rest of the evening? she wondered despairingly.

And—bleaker prospect still—how was she going to get through the rest of her life?

When she finally emerged from the powder-room, the first person her eyes alighted on was Jake.

Her heart felt as if it was going to thump its way right out of her chest as she gazed at him. It was not surprising, of course, that she'd noticed him right away—partly because of his height, partly because of his harshly handsome features and his arrestingly dark hair, but also because of the supreme self-confidence evident in his bearing, the arrogant tilt of his head.

He was standing at the other side of the room, talking with someone she'd never seen before. The man was around seventy, distinguished-looking with grey hair and aquiline features. She stood for a moment, watching curiously as the stranger shook Jake's hand before turning away with the silver-haired woman at his side.

Dragging her gaze away, Briony saw Diane dance by with Robb, and over by the band she noticed Charles and Prue moving sedately round the floor.

She stood there, undecided as to what she should do. She didn't want to go back to the table and sit alone in case Jake came over and asked her to dance. But she didn't want to just stand there like a dummy...

She exhaled a sigh as she noticed Jake was still at the far side of the room...but now he was scanning the throng of dancers. Was he looking for her? She saw him frown, saw him drag an impatient hand through his hair. And then, just as she thought he was going to give up, he turned and saw her. She saw his expression darken, and her throat tightened as she saw him coming towards her. Coming towards her purposefully——

'Excuse me, dear.'

Briony's attention was jolted away from Jake as she realised she was blocking the entrance to the ladies' room. With a murmured apology, she stepped aside, noticing that the woman who wanted to get by was the one whose husband had been talking to Jake a moment ago... and who now was hovering a couple of feet away, looking at a display of silver golfing trophies arranged in a glass-fronted cabinet.

Glancing apprehensively back towards Jake, Briony saw that he had been momentarily waylaid by one of the club attendants. But any moment now he would make for her again.

She stepped across to the stranger. 'Would you care to dance?'

She could hardly believe she had spoken to the tall, grey-haired man. Only when he turned and looked down at her, a smile on his face, did it really sink in.

'Dance? I'd love to.' He nodded towards the ladies' room. 'Sybil has gone in there to "freshen up". Knowing Sybil, I'm sure she'll be all of fifteen minutes—more than enough time for us to get around the floor once or twice.'

It was, Briony knew, only a temporary reprieve. Jake's manners were impeccable, and he wouldn't let the evening pass without inviting her to dance. But a temporary reprieve was all she could hope for, so she took it.

A moment before they were swept up in the crowd Briony caught a brief glimpse of him. He was alone again, a frown of irritation etched on his brow as he scanned the now empty corner where she'd been standing. Then, turning abruptly, he strode away and she saw him go out of one of the side-doors.

'Name's Bartlett Whyte.' Her partner's voice drew her attention back to him. 'Here from London, having a golfing holiday. Staying with the Tremartins,' he added gruffly. 'Know them, my dear?'

'Oh, yes.' Bartlett Whyte...that explained how the man knew Jake. He was a lawyer too. But whereas Jake, with his Bridgeport practice, was a large fish in a comparatively small pool, Bartlett Whyte—senior partner of London's most prestigious law firm, Bartlett Whyte and Richards—was by far the largest fish in Britain's largest pool. 'Are you having a good time?'

'Wonderful...Miss...?'

'Campbell. Briony Campbell.'

'As I was saying, Briony, wonderful. People here are a first-class bunch.' He chuckled. 'Just met someone I hadn't seen in...oh...ten years...and he invited me to play a round with him. Jake Trelawney. Know *him*, my dear?'

Know Jake? A month ago, she'd have said yes, and said it with conviction. Now she found it hard to come up with an answer to satisfy herself, far less this stranger. 'Mm,' she offered, finally. 'We...move in the same circles.'

'Fine man...and a fine mind.' Bartlett Whyte was as skilled a dancer as he was a lawyer. With a flourish, he swept Briony round another couple who were on the verge of bumping into them. 'Matter of fact, more than fine—brilliant. Interviewed him just after he graduated from law school—most promising young man I'd come across in thirty years. Offered him a position with the firm in London.'

Briony felt her eyes widen. A position with Bartlett Whyte and Richards—what a plum! Why had Jake never mentioned this to her? 'But...what happened?'

'Dammit——' Bartlett's pale skin suddenly had a ruddy tinge '—*dammit*, he turned me down!'

'He did?' Confusion had Briony's mind spinning around. 'Why on earth...?'

'The day after his interview his stepmother died. His father had passed away a few months previously, so his stepmother's death left him as guardian to her twelve-year-old daughter. Trelawney insisted that his new ward had been through enough traumas in her life already, without being uprooted and taken to live in the city. He was adamant. Couldn't *budge* him. But I must say that, despite my own deep disappointment, I thought even more highly of the stubborn young whippersnapper because of his selflessness. A rare quality indeed.'

Briony felt as if the cogs in her mind had stopped turning. What was he saying? That...Jake had been offered this incredible chance...and he had turned it down...because of *her*? In a faint voice, she said, 'He articled with a law firm in...Bridgeport... Eventually became a partner——'

'And is now senior partner. Yes, my dear, I know. I kept track of his career... and a very successful one it has been. He's *highly* respected. But I just hope that that young girl, wherever she is now, never led him to regret giving up a once-in-a-lifetime opportunity.'

Briony was vaguely aware that her partner had abruptly changed direction, was vaguely aware that he was saying, 'Ah, there's Sybil. Do come and let me introduce you...'

Briony allowed him to introduce her to his wife, and then, as the couple excused themselves to go and join their hosts, she leaned back against the wall. With an effort, she managed to control the bile that had been rising in her throat ever since Bartlett Whyte had told her about the sacrifice Jake had made. No, she told herself despairingly, it couldn't be true...

How she got back to the table she didn't know. Somehow her feet must have carried her there, and somehow she must have slipped back into her seat. And she must somehow have managed to conceal her distress from the Denhams because when they joined her they didn't seem to notice anything untoward about her appearance.

But, though she might have looked all right on the outside, inside she felt as if she were falling to pieces. So when Charles asked if she'd like something to drink she ordered a gin and tonic, though she'd been having only soft drinks till that point in the evening, apart from a glass of wine with dinner. She drank the gin quite quickly, and in a minute or so began to feel a little less shaky. She had just drained the last drops, and was taking deep breaths in an effort to steady herself, when she felt a tap on her shoulder from behind. She knew it was Jake, though she hadn't seen him come back into the room. She could feel the impact of his presence, feel the surge of electricity that had sizzled through her at his touch. Forcing her features into a controlled mould, she turned round.

'Briony?' He gestured towards the floor and she realised that the band had struck up again.

It was the moment she'd been dreading: Jake's 'duty dance'.

But there was no way of getting out of it, short of being rude... and she could see by the derisive glint in his sapphire eyes that he was expecting her to be just that! With a stiff smile, she got up, and as he cupped her elbow with his fingers his touch on her bare skin sent electrical sensations sizzling through her, sensations so intense that she almost gasped.

She was relieved that at least he'd not asked her to dance while the band was playing something slow and romantic, for then she'd have been trapped in his embrace and might have been unable to hide the effect that his closeness had on her... but that relief quickly changed to panic as he faced her and, thin lips curved in a taunting smile, began moving in time with the fast, pulsating tempo of the music. Romantic it was not... but sensual it undoubtedly was.

Jake was a marvellous dancer—one of those people who seemed to give themselves up entirely to the music, absorbing it into their very being, so that when they moved the result was hypnotic. And, in Jake's case, Briony acknowledged despairingly, not only hypnotic, but *erotic*.

She had danced with him many times in the past, and they had always entered energetically into the spirit of the music. But this was different. Tonight was different. She was different. She was in love with him.

She just couldn't drag her eyes from his face. And as his own gaze, which a moment ago had been mocking, suddenly became hooded, she realised to her horror that she had been so mesmerised by the arrogant masculinity of his movements that she hadn't noticed that she herself had let the power of the music infiltrate her own senses. She hadn't noticed that she was swaying her own hips in a rhythmically seductive manner as the primal beat throbbed through her.

She swallowed, and her throat felt so dry that she thought she would choke. Biting her lip, she felt her body freeze, and she just stood there, barely aware of the music now, or the couples gyrating all around her. She saw Jake frown, but as he leaned forward to say something she spoke first. 'I've had enough—I feel a little dizzy.'

She didn't, but she knew Jake wouldn't force her to keep dancing. He nodded, his eyes narrowed so that she couldn't see their expression. He would take her back to the table now; at the thought, Briony felt a slight lessening of the tension strung so tightly within her.

To her dismay, he grasped her hand firmly and led her towards the French doors. Ignoring her murmur of protest, he drew her out of the clubhouse into the beautiful summer evening, and before she could catch her breath he began walking her along one of the paths criss-crossing the rose-beds situated above the first tee.

'It's hot in there,' he murmured at last. 'You'll be all right in a minute.'

No, she thought despairingly, she wouldn't be all right in a minute; she'd never be all right again. Not now that she knew the truth. Not now that she knew she'd ruined Jake's life, blocked a brilliant career, by the very fact of her existence.

The sob which clutched her throat was so unexpected that she didn't have time to try to fight it back. It came out with a harshness that was an offence to the sweet hush of the garden, and as it faded away she heard the music of the achingly emotional 'Love Me Tender' drift through the rose-scented air, the voluptuous sentiment in the melody widening the crack in her breaking heart. Shakily, she turned away from Jake.

'Are you crying?'

His hands were on her shoulders, then warm fingers were forcing her chin up so that she would have to look at him. She refused to do so, unwilling for him to see the agony in her eyes.

'What's wrong, Bri?' His voice was quiet, the pad of his thumb gentle as he wiped the tears from her lashes.

She hadn't meant to let him know she'd found out what he'd done for her. She knew that if he'd wanted her to know he'd have told her years ago. But the strain she'd been under ever since her return to the Crag caught up with her all of a sudden, and when he put his arms around her, and pulled her firmly against his chest, her anguish drained away all her resolution, and with a low moan she buried her face against his chest.

'Oh, Jake.' Her voice, barely audible, was husky with tears. 'I didn't know...'

'Didn't know what?' His lips brushed her temple, and at his touch the ache in her heart intensified unbearably. 'It's not Price, is it? Finding out that he spent the night with Diane?'

She shook her head. 'No, I've never cared for Tony in that way, despite what you thought...'

'What, then?' he persisted quietly.

'I...I didn't know...what you'd done.' She could feel her tears soaking into his blue sweater, could feel the fine cotton become damp. But she couldn't stop them. Her despair was like a dark and crushing weight, a weight which she was unable to support.

'Oh, Jake,' she whispered, with an effort raising her glistening eyes to look at him as she spoke. 'I didn't know you turned down a job with Bartlett Whyte and Richards when you graduated.'

CHAPTER NINE

IF JAKE hadn't been holding her, Briony wouldn't have been aware that he had stiffened at her words, but he *was* holding her, and she felt his muscles become tight. And she saw him frown. But immediately he seemed to relax again, and when he spoke his voice was steady.

'That's ancient history, Bri.' His breath, fragrant with wine, fanned her face as he kept his gaze fixed on hers. 'But not common knowledge. How did you find out?'

'I...I was dancing with...Bartlett Whyte.' Briony caught her lower lip between her teeth for a moment to stop it trembling. 'He...started talking about you. He didn't connect the two of us, since our surnames are different, and...I didn't tell him who I was...'

For a moment Jake was absolutely still. When he spoke, it was with a studied casualness. 'Oh,' he murmured, 'yes...Bartlett and his wife. They're staying with the Tremartins. We're going to have a game next week——'

'Jake, how can I ever make it up to you? Oh, I know I can't; it's impossible.'

His eyes were suddenly wary. 'Make it up to me?' he said slowly. 'Make *what* up to me?'

He was going to pretend his decision had nothing to do with her! 'Oh, stop it, Jake,' she cried. 'Bartlett said you gave up the chance to work with his firm because you became my guardian——'

'Briony——'

'And you didn't want to disrupt my life by moving me from the Crag——'

'Briony, will you just lis——?'

'Please don't try to deny it, Jake! I know what a sacrifice you made——'

'For God's sake, Bri, stop it!' He shook her, not roughly, but not gently either. Just enough to calm her rising hysteria. 'You're being melodramatic. It wasn't a question of making a sacrifice.' He pronounced each word emphatically. 'It was a question of doing what was best.'

'But if it hadn't been for me you'd have taken the job in London. Oh, Jake, please don't lie to me...not now!'

'No, I won't lie to you.' His dark eyes glittered. 'Yes, Bri, I would have accepted Bartlett's offer——'

'Oh, Jake...' Briony felt as if her heart were being torn apart.

'Let me finish,' he went on, a harsh note creeping into his voice. 'Yes, I would have accepted Bartlett's offer if it hadn't been for you... but I don't ever again want to hear you talk of repaying me for what I did.' He brushed a wisp of damp hair from her brow, gently. 'You had just lost your mother, and you were devastated. I wouldn't have dreamed of uprooting you from the Crag—I wouldn't have dreamed of making you change schools, forcing you to make another set of friends. And I wouldn't have dreamed of going to London alone and leaving you with Poll, for she was virtually a stranger to you when she first came as housekeeper. What you needed more than anything at that time was stability, a sense of continuity.'

'Oh, you gave me that, Jake...and more, much more...'

'Bri, it hasn't been a one-way street! You in turn have enriched my life in so many ways—ways you couldn't possibly imagine. I have never, not even for a second, regretted the choice I made.'

Was it the passionate intensity in his voice... or the caressing movements of his fingers over her hair that caused the needles of electricity to start prickling across her skin? Briony didn't know... but what she *did* know was that now they had started there seemed to be no stopping them. They danced from nerve-ending to nerve-ending all over her body, heating her blood and stimulating deliciously pleasurable feelings in her satin-soft nipples... and from there sliding downwards on sheer silken threads of sensation to gather and knot in the smooth velvet pulse at her core. 'Oh, Jake...' The sound that escaped her was seeking, protesting, like the mew of a tiny kitten.

The moon was full, round, like a great white-yellow paper disc. The scent of roses came, sweet and intoxicating, from the damp-earthed flower-beds. The sound of the music drifting through the air was like a persuasive presence, inciting her senses to riot, inflaming them, till she thought she would die of the hunger in her heart. Lips moist and parted, she felt herself drowning in Jake's eyes. He was so beautiful, so wonderful, the tilt of his head as he looked down at her emphasising the incredible perfection of his features, the hauntingly attractive planes and angles, the wide brow, the strong, chiselled nose, the thin lips...

The thin, *sensual* lips...

She stared at those lips, longing to feel them clinging to her own. Oh, Jake, she pleaded silently, kiss me, please kiss me...

Her mouth went dry as she saw a sudden flare of awareness in his dark blue eyes. Dear God, had she uttered her thoughts aloud? Surely not... but had he seen the invitation in her gaze, the unspoken plea?

He must have, for his expression became swiftly shuttered. And even as she stood gazing up helplessly at him he dropped his hands, and took a step back, his lips twisted in an ironic smile.

Eyes still holding hers, he murmured in a controlled tone, 'So easy to be carried away on such a romantic night, with the moonlight, the wine, and the music... and the scent of summer roses. A heady combination... and a dangerous one.' He slid his hands into his pockets and Briony heard the clink of coins. 'I think, little Bri, that it's time we went inside. People do foolish things on an evening such as this...'

'Foolish things, Jake?' Briony murmured in a thready, trembling voice. 'What... kind of foolish things?'

She shivered as he took one hand out of his pocket and with a faint, distant smile brushed an index finger lightly over the curve of her upper lip. 'Foolish things like... kissing someone they've accused of being a liar?'

It took Briony a moment to assimilate what he had just said. When she did, she drew back with a sharply inhaled breath. How could he shatter such a tender moment between them? But even as she recoiled from him she felt a hot tide of humiliation flood over her. It was all too plain that he had noticed her yearning to be kissed... and all too plain that he was rejecting her.

Again.

She felt a little splash on her cheek, and for a moment she thought she'd shed a tear. But of course it wasn't a tear—it was too cool for that; it was a drop of rain. Glancing up, her heart torn with anguish, she noticed that a black cloud was beginning to drift across the moon, and the sky was darkening.

'It's going to rain.' Somehow she managed to keep her voice from breaking. 'If you'll excuse me, I'm going inside.'

Without waiting for him to respond, she turned and began walking blindly back to the clubhouse. She heard his step on the path behind her, but he made no attempt to stop her, or even to catch up with her. She reached the French doors, and walked inside just as the band's rendition of 'Love Me Tender' was throbbing emotionally to a close.

Immediately they struck up with the 'Blueberry Polka'. Before Jake could take her arm to guide her back to the table, she found herself swept on to the floor by someone she'd known years ago at school, and the boisterous romp gave her the opportunity to gather herself together.

She was thankful for the breathing-space. And by the time her red-faced, sweating partner returned her to her table she was able to curve her lips in a bright smile, and tell everyone—including Jake—what a *wonderful* time she was having!

The summer shower turned out to be the forerunner of one of the worst storms in living memory.

Next day, gale-force winds swept in from the southwest and lashing rain pounded the coast, sending fishing boats and pleasure boats alike scurrying for shelter. Briony spent the morning at the studio, but by lunchtime had to accept that there would be no tourists coming by in such foul weather.

She lit the fire in the drawing-room in a vain attempt to cheer herself up, and for the best part of the afternoon she sat curled up on the window-seat, staring out unseeingly at the wild splendour of the raging sea.

She knew that Polly was sitting in the kitchen, watching through the window as the sluicing rain beheaded her roses and pitilessly lashed her herb garden— and she knew that Jake was at his office, fit to be tied because Polly had phoned earlier to tell him that he wouldn't be able to get home because a flash-flood had washed away one of the local bridges.

No one expected the storm to last long, it was so savage, but day after weary day it raged on. Everything in the area came to a standstill. Tourists stayed away... and Jake was stranded in town. When the TV weatherman announced at last that by Friday they could expect the weather to clear, everyone breathed a sigh of relief.

The weatherman was right. On Friday, at eleven, the sun peeped from behind watery clouds, tentatively, as if uncertain of the reception it would get after such a long absence.

Briony went down to her studio about eleven-thirty. Her heart was heavy as she looked around at her canvases, all sitting forlornly where she'd left them. No tourists had come her way since the road was closed, and she had only a couple of days left before she was due to leave for London. A couple of days left in which to find the rest of the money to make up the amount she had promised the professor. There was no way she could make it now. She had lost far too much time. With a sigh of despair, she took a cloth and began to wipe away some water that had leaked in through a crack in the wall. What was she going to do?

'You look as if someone has stolen your best friend!'

Briony looked round and saw Polly in the doorway, a rake in her hand. Jake's aunt had such a worried look on her face that Briony forced a smile in an effort to allay the older woman's concern. 'Oh, I was just disappointed that the road was closed for so long. I haven't made as much money as I'd hoped.'

'Yes, that was bad luck, dear. Just as it was bad luck that your sign got ripped off the post by vandals.' Polly leaned on the rake. 'It was *such* a relief to me when I returned from Lady Beresford's and saw it was back in place. I completely forgot I'd carted it up to the house and put it in the workshop...' Her voice trailed away as she looked more closely at Briony. 'Are you all right? I hadn't noticed...but you look absolutely ashen! What——?'

'Will you run that by me again, Polly?' Briony's words came out in a thin whisper.

'Run what by you, dear?'

'What you said...about the sign. You mean, my sign at the end of the lane...?'

'Yes, of course, that's the only sign there is, isn't it? That morning when I went to Prue's for the cuttings some teenage louts were parked at the end of our lane, and one of them was fooling around with your sign. I drew up just as he smashed it from the post. Luckily I had my secateurs with me, and I jumped out and charged.' She chuckled. 'They had an old truck, and—

bunch of cowards—they all jumped in and took off. I heaved the sign into my boot, and when I got back from Prue's I put it in the workshop, meaning to pop over to the studio and tell you.' She tutted exasperatedly. 'Then Della phoned, and it floated right out of my mind. But,' she smiled, 'you obviously found it, so no harm was done.'

No harm was done. Briony felt as if her heart was sinking down into a great black crevasse. If only Polly knew... if she only knew the result of her absent-mindedness.

If she only knew that she, Briony, had accused Jake of being a liar!

She had to apologise. She had to make it right with him. And she couldn't wait. She had to tell him today, right now, what a mistake she had made. And she would beg him to forgive her. But would he?

'Bri... dear... what's *wrong*?'

Briony forced a reassuring smile. 'I'm fine, Polly. But I've suddenly remembered something I have to do in town. I have to leave right away.'

'You'll be careful on the road? I know they said on the radio this morning that they've replaced the bridge that was washed away, but do drive slowly.'

'Don't worry, Poll, I'll be careful.'

But even as she spoke her mind was miles ahead of her, thinking of the meeting she was going to have with Jake.

Jake's office was on the main floor of Bridgeport's most impressive granite building. As Briony pushed through the revolving doors and stepped across the foyer, she saw that Kate-Lynn, the receptionist, wasn't at her desk. Briony was glad she wasn't there. At least she wouldn't have to stop and make small talk with her; all she wanted to do was see Jake, put things straight.

His office was down the carpeted hall to the left, and she met no one in the corridor as she hurried towards it. She knocked loudly on the glass door, but, getting no reply, she turned the handle and went in. The outer office was empty. She crossed it, and tapped on the heavy teak door that led to his private quarters.

Again there was no answer. Briony frowned. Pushing open the door, she saw that this room was empty too.

'Jake?' Her voice echoed hollowly back in the quietness, and she instinctively knew that she was alone.

It was months since she'd been here. Now, drawn as if by a magnet, she crossed to the fireplace, and stood looking at the silver-framed picture of herself and Jake which stood at one end of the mantelpiece. Diane had taken it one afternoon a couple of years ago, when the three of them had been on the boat. Jake was wearing nothing but a pair of white shorts and a yachting cap tilted at a jaunty angle; her own shorts were white, and with them she was wearing a pink blouse. Her hair had blown across her face just before the picture was taken, and Diane had captured the moment when Jake was brushing the strands aside, and she was looking up at him, laughter...and adoration...in her eyes.

Pain shafted through her as she recalled the sheer joy she'd felt at that moment, and abruptly she turned away. She knew she would never regain that wonderful rapport she'd once shared with Jake, not after the dreadful accusation she'd hurled at him.

But she had to try.

Kate-Lynn was back at her desk when Briony came out of Jake's office, but she was rummaging about in the bottom drawer while talking to someone on the phone. 'I'm sorry, Dick——' her voice was muffled '—he's gone out for lunch. No, he said he'd be back around two. He's just next door at the Pelican.'

Unseen, Briony slipped out to the street, and a moment later she was walking up the steps in front of the Pelican Hotel.

The place was bustling with activity, and no one paid her any attention as she entered the crowded foyer. The dining-room was ahead, to her right, and she felt her heart give a great lurch when she saw Jake coming from there. It was days since she'd seen him, and, hardly realising what she was doing, she halted abruptly, beside a wide white pillar, staring at him.

He was wearing his black leather jacket, dark trousers, and a black turtle-neck sweater. His hair was a little too long, his face a little too drawn. Tall, brooding, intense, he was turning every female head in the lobby. But he seemed not to notice.

He began to walk across the foyer, in her direction, but obviously not having seen her yet. Briony swallowed, and was about to take a step forward, when she saw Jake's expression change. It lightened... his lips curved in a smile, his eyes lit up warmly. Briony followed his gaze... and saw a slender redhead approaching him from the direction of the powder-room, her mouth curved in a tentative smile. She was wearing a loose tomato-red sweater, and a pair of cream trousers. Not the kind of person to stand out in a crowd, but lovely in a quiet, understated way, and as Briony stared at her she felt her mind scramble to make sense of what she was seeing.

No, it couldn't be... For a moment Briony thought she was mistaken—but only for a moment. There could be only one person with that shy smile, that beautiful auburn hair.

Jake's companion was Angelique St Clair.

Every cell in Briony's body became paralysed. She stood there, unable to move, staring while Jake put an arm round Angelique's shoulders, his blue eyes focused intently on her, his lips moving as he murmured words that Briony couldn't hear. It was obvious that at this moment no one else existed for him. And, as Briony gazed incredulously, she recalled what Jake had said to her just the week before.

'The woman of my choice? She's young, and innocent. And she's very beautiful.'

They were only ten feet from her before Briony, in a sudden panic, realised that they were going to see her any second. Glancing wildly around, she noticed to her dismay that the foyer, which a moment ago had been crowded, was now almost empty. The only place she could hide was behind the pillar.

Swiftly, she stepped sideways, and slid round to the other side of it, leaning back to support herself as her legs threatened to give way under her. She closed her eyes, and prayed that her hiding place would be adequate.

Her pulses staggered as she heard Jake's crisp tread on the marble floor, echoed by the light click of Angelique's sandals. Her mouth went dry as she heard the hum of their conversation, her breath choked in her throat as she caught a whiff of a musky, mossy perfume...the same perfume as the one that had drifted to her nostrils from the silky scarf in Jake's car...

And she felt her heart stop as she realised that the couple had paused by the pillar.

'You'll tell Briony?' There was no mistaking Angelique's soft, slightly hesitant voice—and the moment Briony heard it, it was like a light bulb going on in her brain. All at once, everything clicked into place. How could she have been so dense? *Angelique* was the woman who had phoned Jake, *Angelique* was the woman with the oh, so tantalisingly familiar voice...

And there weren't two mysterious women in Jake's life after all. The redhead with the perfumed scarf, and the woman with the husky, hesitant voice were one and the same. Angelique St Clair.

In a daze, Briony realised Jake was now talking.

'Yes, I'll tell her.'

'Tonight? I'd hate her to hear from someone else.'

'Yes, tonight. As soon as I get home. It'll be a load off my mind, not having to keep it from her. And now that you've said, "Yes"——'

'I'm sorry I took so long—but I know in my heart that I've made the right decision——'

'And one I promise you you'll never regret.' Jake's tone was warm, protective.

'How do you think she'll take it, when you tell her?'

'Badly.' Jake's voice had become hard.

Angelique sighed. 'Yes, I guess she'll be devastated. Oh, I feel so sorry for her. It hurts when your dreams are shattered...'

Whatever Jake's response was, Briony couldn't hear it because they had moved on. But she was beyond hearing anything more anyway. There was such a buzzing in her head that she put both hands to her temples in an attempt to clear it, but in vain.

Jake... and Angelique...

Why had he never mentioned that he knew her? Why had he kept their relationship a secret? Had he been waiting till he cleared things up with Diane? At any rate, it seemed that he and Angelique had put all their problems behind them. She had finally said 'Yes'. It was the lovely redhead, not Diane, whom Jake planned to marry.

'It hurts when your dreams are shattered.'

Shame was like a great black cloud enveloping Briony as the words echoed in her head. Oh, what an idiot she'd been! To have fallen so hard for Jake... and to have let him see how she felt. How painfully embarrassing it must have been for him to have to watch her reaction to him whenever they were together. Oh, how was she going to face him now?

For face him she would have to. His secret was going to be a secret no longer. He was going to come home tonight to tell her that Angelique was the woman of his choice.

She didn't think she could bear it.

'A letter for you, dear!' Polly stood at the front door, frantically waving a long envelope as Briony walked across the gravel from the Lollipop. 'And you'll *never* guess who it's from!'

'No.' Briony tried to sound bright and cheerful. 'I'm sure I shan't... so are you going to tell me?'

'It's from Dorothy Marsden!' Polly's eyes shone with excitement as she handed over the letter. '*Dorothy Marsden*! When did you meet her, Bri? How thrilling!'

'Dorothy Marsden? Surely not *the* Dorothy Marsden?' As she and Polly walked across the front hall together, Briony examined the name and return address on the envelope, a frown gathering between her eyebrows. 'I don't know her, Polly—though I feel as if I do! I used to love her books when I was a little girl.' Curiosity making her impatient, she ripped open the envelope. Inside was a flimsy, typed letter. 'Let's go into the drawing-room.'

As they moved through the doorway, Briony skimmed the contents of the letter, reading them aloud for Polly's benefit, her voice becoming more and more incredulous the further she went.

'Dear Ms Campbell,

I am writing to thank you for the sketch you so kindly gave me when I visited your studio. I can now explain my interest in your intriguingly life-like animal drawings.

As you may know, I write children's books, and I have been commissioned by my publisher, Coe and Blackberry, to write a series of nature books. Each book will be set in a different English county, using the creatures of the area as fictional characters around which the tales will be woven. The first county I am to tackle is Cornwall. I have been searching for an illustrator for the series, but until I saw your exquisitely detailed sketches I had not found someone with exactly the right touch. You have a rare talent and imagination, and I find your drawings wonderfully appealing. You not only succeed splendidly in conveying the beauty and peace of the outdoors in the delicate lines of your work, but at the same time you reveal in the facial expressions of your characters your caring and tenderness towards them. I think what touches me more than anything, however, is your delightful sense of humour...'

Briony stopped abruptly, gazing in disbelief at the rest of the letter.

'Go on, dear!' Polly's voice was high with excitement. 'Do go on!'

Briony sank down into one of the low armchairs by the hearth and quickly read to the end. 'I'd have to be available in September. She wants me to phone her immediately if I'm interested, then meet her in London at the Coe and Blackberry offices to sign a contract...' Leaning back, eyes closed, she went on, 'The advance the publisher offers...oh, dear God, Polly...I can't take it all in! Here——' she held out the letter '—read it for yourself.'

'Dorothy Marsden came to your studio? She was here, at the Crag? Oh, my lord! What did she look like?' Polly shook her head as she read the letter. 'Did she have a halo and a white-spangled dress, and a shiny silver wand? Did she *look* like the kind of person who can perform miracles?'

Briony laughed. 'No, Poll...actually she was plump and plain, and wore glasses. Very nice, though...' Nice? That was the understatement of the year. All at once, as the full impact of the offer registered on Briony's brain, she felt an almost overwhelming surge of relief. She didn't have to stay here and face Jake—she would phone Dorothy Marsden this afternoon, and arrange to meet her in London tomorrow. She'd set off before Jake came home tonight.

And she'd be leaving for Paris the day after tomorrow with Professor Sharp and his wife. Surely, by the time she came back, she'd have begun to get over the pain of knowing Jake belonged to someone else.

But first there was something she had to do.

Polly knew that she was planning to go away for the month of August, but she, Briony, had been purposefully vague about her holiday plans. Now she must tell her she was going abroad.

'Poll.' She got up and linked an arm through one of Polly's. 'I have something to tell you. Let's go through to the kitchen and make a cup of tea, and you can let me know what you'd like me to bring you home from Paris.'

It was almost five before she got under way. It had taken her longer than she expected to pack, and then at the last minute she had to wait while Jake's aunt wrote out a cheque to pay an overdue bill.

'Will you pop it in a letter-box on your way to the station, dear? It won't take a moment, and it'll save me going out. Now, I know you want to get going,' Polly smiled, her eyes misting with tears, 'and I won't keep you. Are you sure you can't wait to say goodbye to Jake?'

'I saw him when I was in town, Polly.' It was a white lie—she was implying that she had talked with him, but of course she hadn't. 'Now, I really must be off.'

'You'll be leaving the Lollipop at Bridgeport Garage and walking across to the station...'

Briony slammed the boot shut on her two cases. Polly had assumed she was going to London by train; she wasn't looking for a response to her comment, and Briony didn't offer her one. Instead, she turned and gave the older woman a warm hug. 'Take care, Poll. I'll send you oodles of postcards.' Getting into the car, she rolled down the window. 'I'm off now.' She started the engine. '*Au revoir*.' She grinned and waved as she drew away.

'*Au revoir*...'

Polly's smile was watery, and in the rear-view mirror Briony could see her lingering at the front door. Then she guided the red Volkswagen around the corner in the lane, and Polly was lost to view.

But someone else was coming towards her. Jake. In his silver Jaguar. His face was taut as he backed to the end of the narrow lane so that they could ease by each other.

He rolled down his window. 'Where are you going?' His tone was terse. 'I need to talk to you.'

Oh, yes, Jake, I know you need to talk to me, and I know what you want to say. But I don't want to hear it. I don't want to hear you tell me you're in love with Angelique! 'We can talk later, Jake. I'm in a bit of a rush right now.'

'Where are you going?' he repeated.

Briony knew she was lying by omission and she crossed her fingers before saying, 'Polly asked me to post a letter for her... actually it's a bill that's overdue. She wants it to catch the mail.'

Jake tapped his fingers impatiently on his steering-wheel. 'All right. But when you get back, come and see me. It's very important, Bri.'

Briony let her car begin to roll away. 'All right. I'll see you when I get back. Bye.' Pressing her foot to the accelerator, she wheeled from the lane on to the highway, hoping he hadn't noticed the tears welling in her eyes. He would find out, as soon as he talked with Polly, that she had tricked him. He would be angry; he hated deception. He might even come after her. But that was all right. He would never find her.

A moment later she checked her rear-view mirror and did a quick U-turn before speeding back the way she'd just come. She knew she had fooled Jake, knew he had watched her take off in the direction of Bridgeport. She laughed, a mirthless sound; she had never had any intention of going to London by train. She was going to drive. So if, after talking with Polly, he stormed into Bridgeport in the Jag to look for her, he wouldn't find her. And by the time he realised what had happened she would be many miles away on the highway, on the first lap of her long journey.

* * *

London was baking hot. The pavements seemed to burn right through the soles of her sandals as she walked dazedly along the street after leaving the imposing Coe and Blackberry offices. Exhilaration rippled through her as she clutched her shoulder-bag against her hip. The cheque was tucked inside her wallet, and though she had seen it with her own two eyes she could still scarcely believe her luck. When she added it to the money already in her account—the money she'd made from the earlier sale of her canvases—she had more than enough to settle her bill with Professor Sharp.

It had been such a long, tiring month, she reflected. It would be good to get away, to put all the tension, the unpleasantness behind her. She couldn't wait to get on that plane!

And when she returned from her trip she would go back to the Crag and pack up all her possessions. Then she would move out, before Jake brought Angelique home.

CHAPTER TEN

WHERE on earth were the Sharps?

Restlessly, Briony looked across the crowded boarding lounge for the hundredth time, and breathed a sigh of relief when, finally, she saw the professor striding towards her.

'Thank *goodness*,' she said with a shaky laugh as he reached her. 'Another ten minutes or so, and I'd have been on my way to Paris alone. I was beginning to panic!'

'Lord, I'm sorry, Briony.' He swept his thin hair back from his brow. 'I had the devil of a job finding a spot in the long-term car park.'

Briony looked past him, her eyes bright with expectancy. She had never met Mrs Sharp, and she was looking forward to being introduced to her. 'Your wife? She's——'

'Ladies and gentlemen,' the announcement came over the Tannoy, 'we shall now board passengers in seats thirteen to twenty-six.'

A firm hand gripped Briony's arm. 'You picked up your ticket?'

'Yes, but——'

'Good. That's us, then. We're in row fourteen—I managed to get you a window-seat. It's——'

'But your wife... shouldn't we wait for her?' Briony shook her head confusedly. 'I'm sorry... Where is she?'

A regretful look passed over the professor's pale features. 'Celine, I'm afraid, won't be able to come with us. Unfortunately, all our careful planning went awry this afternoon when she found out that her very dearest friend is gravely ill in hospital. Celine rushed to her bedside, where she is now. Though I offered to stay with her, she insisted I must go. She knew how very much this trip meant to you.'

What was he saying? Briony slid her elbow from his grip, and stepped away from him. She felt trembly, the way she did when she was coming down with something. 'You mean...you and I will be travelling *alone* together?'

He gave a short laugh. 'You're surely not worried about travelling without a chaperon? In this day and age? We're both adults...surely we don't need to be concerned with what people might think?'

'No...' Briony spoke slowly, trying to clear the fog that seemed to be clouding her brain. 'No, I've never concerned myself with what people might think, as long as I know I'm doing what's right.' But was this right, what he was suggesting?

'It's not as if I planned this, Briony!' His tone was gently mocking, but as Briony looked into his eyes she saw in them a bland expression which sent a strange little shiver scurrying through her. It was that same expression she'd seen there that evening when she'd gone to his home, when she'd thought he'd made a pass at her. She had swiftly dismissed the idea.

But now...

He reached out to take her arm. The voice on the Tannoy was saying, 'Boarding seats one to twelve...' The sound echoed round and round in Briony's head.

She pulled away from him. 'I can't go.' Despite her best efforts to keep the words steady, there was a distinct tremor in her voice. 'I can't go. Not if your wife isn't coming with us.'

'I suspected that would be your first reaction.' His words flowed sweetly, like warm treacle. 'But be practical, my dear. This trip has cost a lot of money—money that is not refundable. If you back out now...' His shrug made it more clear than words that she'd have to be a fool to throw all that money away. 'Briony, what harm is there in it? We have separate rooms in each of the hotels we'll be staying in. You do trust me, don't you?'

As he spoke the words, they acted like a trigger, setting off a train of thought in Briony's brain. Reminding her of someone else who had asked her not too long ago if she trusted him...

'For God's sake, Bri, I've told you in no uncertain terms that I don't want you to go on this trip! I'm thinking only of what's best for you. Can't you trust me?'

And what had she replied? 'Trust you? I've always trusted you, Jake.'

And it was true. She *had* always trusted Jake. She *had* always known that he wanted only what was best for her. If she'd listened to him in the first place, this would never have happened. She'd never have landed herself in this predicament, where she had to offend the professor...

Because offend him she must.

And why was she so sure? Because when he said, 'You do trust me, don't you?' her instincts, sadly, told her no.

'I am really sorry.' Her words came out in a whisper, though she'd tried to make them strong. 'I hate to back out, and of course I hate to sacrifice the money, but——'

'Excuse me——' An airport official in a navy and red uniform appeared beside them, frowning. 'Is there some problem? The plane will be leaving in a few minutes.'

'We'll be right there.' The professor dismissed the man with an abrupt gesture and grasped Briony's arm, pulling her into a corner. 'Don't do this, Briony.' His voice was low but insistent, his eyes glittering. 'Don't be a fool.'

Briony felt a great lump rise in her throat. 'I wanted to go on this trip with you more than anything in the world. It was a dream come true.'

She felt his fingertips dig into her flesh. 'You don't have to keep up this act any longer. I know you want to come with me—I've known all along that you liked me.

You knew damned well that my wife wasn't coming—we didn't have to put it in so many words.'

Briony stared at him disbelievingly. 'No,' she said hoarsely, 'I didn't know. And you're wrong about me. That's not the kind of person I am. But I was wrong about you too. I thought you were someone special, someone I could look up to, someone I could learn from.'

His breath was hot on her cheek as he pulled her against him. She could feel his hard outline against her stomach, and she felt horror shaft through her as she realised what his body was telling her. Right here, out in the open, where anyone could see them! Shame spilled over inside her, mingling with disgust and loathing.

'You filthy beast!' She tore herself from him, her cheeks scarlet, her body shuddering. 'You're...' She shook her head, unable to continue, as tears of humiliation and shock scalded her eyes and blocked her throat. Tearing open her bag, she fumbled for the cheque, and thrust it at him. She didn't feel even one twinge of regret as the money left her hands—it was a small price to pay for the lesson she had learned. He knew what it was; he didn't even look at the cheque as he snatched it. They stared at each other for a moment that seemed endless to Briony, the tension between them so intense that she could almost feel it screaming.

Then, gathering up all her remaining strength, she whirled away from him.

She heard him swear harshly and insultingly as she began to walk away across the lounge, and she felt as if her skin were crawling. Her trainers made a soft slapping sound on the tiled floor, her bag thumped painfully against her hip as she walked quickly out into the hallway, and then she could hear nothing except the painful, noisy rasping of her own breath.

The death of her dream.

The phrase rang in her head, and she remembered that it was that same phrase which had rung in her head when she'd run so furiously after Jake that afternoon on the moor. How foolish to have been so infatuated with the idea of the proposed trip that she hadn't listened to him then, listened to his advice.

She choked back a painful sob. The only dream worth having was a dream that involved Jake.

And that was a dream that was never to be.

What was she to do now?

Briony, a mug of coffee cupped in her hands, stared bleakly into space, oblivious of the clamour all around her in the airport's vast cafeteria.

Her options, she realised, were few. She had an old school friend who lived in Potter's Bar, and she could phone her and ask if she could stay with her for a while, but she really didn't feel up to explaining why; and if she checked in at a hotel, as she had last night, her money would soon run out—and of course she didn't even have a change of clothes; her cases at this very moment would be on their way across the Channel.

And she didn't want to return to the Crag and face Jake. Not yet. She wasn't ready to hear him tell her that he was in love with Angelique. She smiled bitterly; would she ever be ready for that? The way she felt now, she didn't think she would.

Wearily she got to her feet and tossed her empty plastic cup into a bin. She had always wondered how it would feel to be in love; now she knew. It was agony. Sheer agony. She brushed the back of a hand across her eyes as she felt unwelcome tears welling—her heart was filled with images of Jake; he was a part of her, and had been for as long as she could remember.

Swallowing back the huge lump in her throat, she made her way through the swarms of travellers. The people were all shapes and sizes, but through her blurred eyes she noted that one person stood out in the crowd. Much taller than anyone else, his hair much darker than anyone else's, the man was striding by about fifteen feet away, and the crowd seemed to part for him the way the Red

Sea parted for Moses. Briony felt her heartbeats stagger; for a moment she had thought it was Jake. He had the same arrogant tilt to his head, the same wide shoulders...

The same blue shirt. The same as the one Diane had given Jake at Christmas.

Barely knowing what she was doing, Briony began following the man. Her gaze riveted to the back of his head, she bumped her way through the crowd, grimacing apologetically and muttering 'Sorry' when she stepped on someone's toes or knocked someone off-balance. There was no doubt it was Jake; and there was no doubt why he was here. He had come after her.

Someone rammed into her from behind, and she turned involuntarily to find a woman in a sari smiling in apology. Nodding distractedly, Briony turned back, and halted abruptly as she saw that Jake had disappeared. She clicked her tongue despairingly, and pushed her way past a trolley, to find herself at the end of a bank of telephone cubicles. And as she whirled round, her face screwed up in a frustrated grimace, she caught sight of Jake again.

He was in one of the open cubicles, about ten feet from where she stood, and she had a side view of him. The phone was at his ear, his lean features were set in dark, haggard lines, and he was feeding money into the machine. Feeling as if she no longer had any control of her actions, Briony found herself moving towards him like a robot as he punched out a series of numbers. Clutching the strap of her shoulder-bag, she stared at this man she loved, drinking in every aspect of his being. Adoring every aspect of his being. Adoring the silky black hair, overlong and curling at his nape, the strong nose and determined chin, the finely moulded mouth...

She was so close now, she could hear him.

'She's gone, Polly. Dammit to hell, I got held up for hours in the traffic when two buses collided and I missed her. By the time I found out which flight she was on——'

He broke off for a moment, listening, and then he said in a harsh tone, 'Yes, I know they're not supposed to discuss passenger lists, Poll, but I have a connection. It just took longer than I'd anticipated. She's gone. She and Sharp both checked in.'

He paused again. 'No.' His voice was even harsher. 'His wife did not. Poll, I'm going to Paris...'

Another brief pause, then he said, 'No, that's going to be too late. I'm going to rent a private plane... Look, I've got to go, Poll...I just wanted you to know...'

'Jake...' Briony hadn't meant to speak; the word just slipped from between her parted lips. But once said there was no pulling it back.

She saw Jake's shoulders stiffen. For a second he froze, his whole body froze, and then he jerked his head round.

His gaze met Briony's, and for a moment she felt as if the floor were tilting under her feet, the way the deck did on *Trelawney's Woman* when it heeled over in a strong sea. His eyes were burning with a savage fire that sent a shiver coursing through her...a shiver of apprehension. Oh, lord, she'd never seen him this way before...she would never, in a million years, have guessed that he was capable of such fury. His face was contorted with it. Raking a harsh gaze over her, from top to toe, taking in her dishevelled hair, her pale face, her casual shirt and jeans, he inhaled a shuddering breath.

And then he turned back to the phone. 'Are you still there, Polly?' After a slight pause, he went on, 'Good. She's here... Yes... Briony. She's here. She hadn't left yet after all. There must have been a hitch. No.' His tone became even more taut, more savage. 'No, I shan't let her go this time.'

Dear God, surely her legs weren't going to give way...surely her humiliation was intense enough, without her having to suffer the further ignominy of fainting dead away. Willing herself to stand straight, Briony waited for him to focus his full attention on her.

She didn't have to wait long.

He turned again, and this time his eyes were as hard as the granite at the Crag. 'Where's your car?'

'In the long-term car park,' she somehow managed.

'It'll be all right there. I'll have it picked up later and delivered. Give me that——' Roughly he relieved her of her flight bag. 'And let's, for God's sake, get out of here.'

'Jake, I have to tell you... the professor——'

'Damn the professor!' Jake exploded. 'He can spend the rest of his life in this airport looking for you for all I care. You can forget about him, and you can forget about the trip. You're coming with me!'

Briony winced as he curled his fingers in a steely clamp around her wrist. Jake, of course, couldn't know what had happened... he assumed that she was still planning to leave. Assumed that she and Professor Sharp had just temporarily gone their separate ways. She would have to tell him what happened... had been going to, just then, before he had interrupted her. She was glad he'd interrupted her—if she'd started to explain, she probably would have broken down. Explanations could come later. And apologies.

She drew in a shaky breath, and allowed him to draw her towards the exit. 'Where... where are you taking me?'

He didn't answer.

A few minutes later they were outside, and the Jag was rolling up at the kerb. Jake tipped the valet driver, before thrusting Briony peremptorily into the passenger seat.

And as she sank back in the low leather cushions, exhausted and fighting back her rising sobs, she heard him say tersely, as if to himself, 'I'm taking you home.'

The only light showing at the Crag when they arrived was the outside light at the front door. It was obvious that Polly hadn't waited up—confident that Briony, now she was once more with Jake, was safe.

Drained of every last vestige of energy, Briony leaned weakly against the wall as Jake inserted the large key in the lock and opened the door. Wordlessly, she walked past him into the hall, and then just stood there, waiting for him to lash out at her. He hadn't spoken at all as they drove through the night, perhaps because she herself, hoping to avoid an unpleasant confrontation, had lain back with her eyes shut, pretending to be asleep. She had in fact dozed off only once, and then briefly; her mind was in too much of a turmoil to let her relax.

Now, despite her utter exhaustion, she felt herself tense as Jake clicked the door shut behind him and switched on the hall light. His anger—heated and savage—filled the space between them, pulsing relentlessly. Briony braced herself for whatever it was that he was going to say.

'Why did you lie to me?' He flung her flight bag down on the floor and strode over to where she was standing, his eyes boring into her like laser beams. 'Why did you tell me you were going to post a letter for Polly?'

Oh, lord, he was going away back to that... A quivering sigh escaped her. 'Polly *did* ask me to——'

'You know what I mean,' he said harshly. 'Why did you leave for London without telling me where you were going? I think I deserve better than that, to have you sneaking away without so much as a goodbye.'

Pain twisted inside Briony. Of course he deserved better than that—this man, this kind and generous man, who had always looked out for her, from the moment she had become his ward. Dear God, she had made a mess of things! Tears of remorse welled up in her eyes, and to hide them from him she turned away. 'I'm sorry.' There was a choking sound to her words. 'It was unforgivable.'

'No.' The hard voice came from right behind her, and hard fingers dug into her shoulders, forcing her round to face him again. 'No, Briony, not unforgivable... not if you had a reason for your actions. Did you—did you have a reason?' His eyes, dark, glittering with some primal emotion, trapped hers, demanding a response.

Yes, she longed to cry out, yes, I had a reason. I left without saying goodbye because I couldn't bear to hear you tell me you were in love with Angelique...

But she didn't want him to know that. 'I didn't trust you,' she said wearily. 'You didn't want me to go on the trip with Professor Sharp, and I was afraid that if you knew I was on my way to London, to meet him, you would try to stop me——' His grip tightened and she uttered a protesting little cry. 'Jake, please...'

Her throat had almost closed, clogged with tears, and she felt a warm tear smear her pale cheek. Closing her eyes in a vain effort to shut out the agony of unhappiness tearing through her, she felt his grip slacken but she was still his prisoner.

'There are some things you have to know——' his voice was rough, grating as rock grinding on rock '—but now, when you're so overwrought, is not the right time to tell you. We'll talk in the morning. Get off to bed now.'

There would never be a 'right time', Briony thought wretchedly as she stumbled away from him and pulled herself up the stairs. There never would be a 'right time' to hear that Jake was in love with Angelique. She had tried to put off the moment by going to London, but tomorrow there would be no escape. She would just have to brace herself, and try to appear happy for Jake's sake. It wouldn't be easy, she acknowledged as she opened her bedroom door and moved across to the bed without putting on the light, but she would do her best.

She was still sitting on the edge of her bed half an hour later, staring mindlessly into space, when she heard Jake's heavy tread on the landing, followed by the sound of his bedroom door opening, and then clicking shut.

The sky was clear, the moon bright, its light shining across the carpet, making it look white. She got up and walked to the uncurtained window, and, leaning against the frame, looked out over the ocean. Endless, and endlessly surging, it made her feel tiny and unimportant. It drew her, pulled at her like a magnet, its beauty and power touching her soul. Her restless soul.

She would never sleep. Not here. Not in this bedroom, with Jake just down the hall.

Through the open window she heard the rhythmic music of the surf as the breakers beat over and over against the rocks and surged with deep sighs across the white sands.

As if in a trance, she moved across to her wardrobe and took out a hooded black sweatshirt. It would be cold down there, by the water. She would need something to keep her warm. And if, by chance, Jake happened to look out of his bedroom window, he wouldn't see her in the moonlight...or if he did see the dark figure gliding across the patio and down the steep steps to the beach he would think it was a shadow.

Slipping the cosy garment over her head, she crossed quickly to the door.

The gull wheeled in the air, crying out harshly before swooping down into the ocean for his lunch.

The sound woke Briony. Drowsily, she raised her arm, and through half-opened eyelids peered at her watch with bleary eyes. Almost twelve.

Almost twelve? *Noon*?

Good grief! Muttering under her breath, she sat up abruptly, and winced as her head hit something hard. Rubbing her scalp, she glared up, and as she saw the panelled bulkhead above her she recollected immediately where she was.

She was on *Trelawney's Woman*.

Dawn had been breaking as she'd reached the beach. She'd found the sea breeze far colder than she'd expected and, shivering, she'd been on the point of climbing back up the steep flight of steps—reluctantly—when she'd thought of the yacht.

The boathouse was kept unlocked, and she had made her along the short jetty, and clambered aboard. It was much warmer down below, and she had taken off the black sweatshirt and curled up on the bunk in the aft cabin. She hadn't meant to fall asleep... but—she grimaced wryly—she obviously had! Perhaps it had been the motion of the yacht on the gently swelling waves, perhaps it had just been sheer exhaustion. Whatever, she had drifted quickly into a deep sleep, and might have dozed for a few more hours, had that screeching gull not decided to give her a raucous wake-up call!

Pushing her tousled blonde hair back from her cheeks, she swung her legs over the edge of the bunk and let out a heavy sigh. She would have to go up to the house now, and face Jake. He would be thinking she was still in bed—thinking, perhaps, that she was too cowardly to come down?—and he would be waiting, fuming with impatience, for her to make her appearance.

The porthole was curtained, and absently she pulled back the rough fabric. Sun blazed through the thick glass; it was obviously another glorious day——

Briony stared disbelievingly as it suddenly registered on her mind that what she was looking out at was not the inside wall of the boathouse, but... land.

She could see the Crag in the distance, perched high on the rocky bluff, and it looked like a toy. She could see the steps leading down to the beach, and they looked like a miniature ladder. She could see the boathouse... and it was miles away.

She was out at sea! What had happened? Had the yacht slipped its moorings...?

Fighting back a surge of panic, she ran across the small cabin and leaped like a gazelle up the companionway steps. Sails billowed above her head, snow-white against the brilliant blue sky, and a gull—the one which had awakened her? Briony wondered fleetingly—wheeled past with something in its beak. But though Briony noticed these things they were all blanked out of her mind a fraction of a second later. Standing at the wheel, with the sun glinting on him so that he looked like a gilded giant, was Jake. He wasn't looking ahead, but sideways, and she could see his profile. Briony felt as if a cruel hand were clenching her heart as she saw the taut, haggard set of his lean features.

He was wearing a navy blue shirt and a pair of white shorts, and his legs were braced to offset the gentle swaying of the yacht. With his black hair blowing in the breeze, his wide shoulders drawn back rigidly, and the muscles of his strong, tanned arms rippling as he grasped the wheel, he looked so devastatingly male and attractive that Briony felt as if her bones were liquefying. Swallowing to relieve the tightness of her throat muscles, she clutched the brass rail at her side, and stood there, as if frozen, her legs refusing to obey her order to take her back again to the safety of the cabin.

'Ah, you're finally awake.'

Jake's steady voice startled her out of her paralysis. She blinked, and saw that he had turned his head, and was looking down at her.

'Yes,' she said in a strangled tone, 'yes, I'm finally awake. I was surprised——' with a supreme effort she managed a wry little laugh '—to find that I had been kidnapped while I was asleep. Where are you taking me?'

'This,' Jake said, 'is as far as we go. I'm going to drop anchor.' His expression was shuttered as he glanced first at her sleep-tumbled hair, and then at her crumpled shirt and creased jeans. 'While I'm making breakfast, you can have a shower.'

She was glad of the opportunity to get away from him...glad of the opportunity to delay the talk that she knew they were going to have...

As she rubbed her hair dry with a thick terry towel after her shower, the aroma of coffee filtered to her nostrils, along with the tantalising smell of frying bacon. She knew Jake would set up their breakfast on deck— he always had done in the past when the day was hot and sunny. Unhappily, she rummaged in the cupboard for clean clothes, and, finding an old pair of yellow shorts and a white T-shirt, she slipped them on.

With a sigh, she moved to the mirror and wove her damp hair back from her face with her fingers. How pale she looked—as if, while she slept, all the blood had drained away from her cheeks. Her eyes had lost their sparkle, and her skin seemed to be too tightly drawn over her cheekbones, as if it had shrunk and didn't fit her any longer. She might as well have been a ghost...

Inhaling a deep breath in an unsuccessful attempt to steady her nerves, she made her way up to the cockpit.

Jake got up briefly from his seat when he saw her, and her heartbeats accelerated when she noticed he'd stripped off the shirt he'd been wearing earlier, and the sun was beating down mercilessly on his naked, muscular shoulders. The black hair covering his chest glistened with sweat, and Briony found her gaze sliding down to where the silky curls formed a V into the low waistband of his shorts. Tearing her eyes away with an effort, she sat as far from him as possible at the opposite side of the table on which he'd arranged a tray.

Strangely, now that they were together, she wanted nothing more than that he broach the subject which she knew was on his mind, and get it over with. She couldn't bear the suspense any longer. If he didn't bring the matter up right away, *she* would...

And when she saw the rich yellow egg yolks running messily into the rashers of crisply cooked bacon she saw the perfect opportunity to give him an opening.

'The woman in your life,' she said lightly, 'should teach you how to fry eggs.' Reaching for the Thermos of coffee, she filled the two large mugs in front of her and, breath caught in her throat, she waited for his response.

CHAPTER ELEVEN

JAKE waited till Briony had taken one of the mugs, and then he took the other. Cupping his large hands around it, he looked at her through the steam rising from the coffee. His eyes had an expression she'd never seen there before... an expression that she found hard to interpret, but if pushed she'd have had to say it was a mixture of pain, anger, and something else—perhaps despair.

'The woman in my life.' His voice had a hard edge. 'Is there a woman in my life, Briony?'

She stared at him, taken aback. What a strange question. Why on earth was he asking her if there was a woman in his life? Unable to meet the diamond-sharp glitter of his penetrating scrutiny, she glanced down at her mug. Had he, somehow, found out that she'd seen him with Angelique at the Pelican? Surely not. Uncomfortably, she shifted on her seat. 'Why did you kidnap me, Jake?' Coward, she thought contemptuously, changing the subject like that!

His thin mouth twisted in a derisive smile, as if he could read her thoughts and agreed with them. But he didn't challenge her. 'Kidnapping you was unintentional, I assure you.' He sipped from his mug. 'This morning I waited for you to come down for breakfast. When there was no sign of you, Poll checked your room around ten and found your bed hadn't been slept in...and I thought...'

'Thought what?' Briony looked up at him bewilderedly.

'I thought you'd taken off.' His jaw tightened. 'I went after you in the Jag, thinking perhaps you were hitch-hiking——'

'Hitch-hiking? But that's so dangerous nowadays! And where on earth would I be hitch-hiking to?'

His wide shoulders moved in an abrupt shrug. 'God knows,' he said tersely. 'I thought I'd frightened you last night, thought I was too hard on you. Finally, I had to face the fact that if you wanted to hide from me I would just have to let you go. I decided to go for a sail——' there was a gravelly tightness to his voice '— and try to blow the cobwebs from my mind, try to make sense of everything that has been happening between us. Shortly after I got under way, I discovered you asleep in the aft cabin.'

She didn't need to ask if he had been relieved; it was evident in the way he shook his head involuntarily, the way he rubbed his nape with a weary hand.

'Polly,' she murmured, 'you've contacted her? She knows... where I am now?'

He nodded. 'She knows.'

'Why... didn't you... turn back... after you found me?'

'As I said last night—or rather, early this morning— I have something to tell you. Something I find it difficult to talk about... and something you'll undoubtedly find very upsetting. What better place to talk than out here——' he waved an all-encompassing hand towards the sparkling blue sea that surrounded them '—where we won't be disturbed?'

Lashes dropped to cover the expression in her eyes, Briony lifted her fork and toyed with her bacon. 'Jake,' she said quietly, 'I already know what you want to tell me.'

In the silence that followed her confession she could hear the breeze whispering in the rigging, the waves splashing against the hull.

'That's impossible, Briony. There's only one other person who knows——'

Yes, she thought miserably. Angelique. Of course she would know! She was the 'woman in his life'!

'I eavesdropped.' Forcing herself to meet his gaze, she saw confusion in the sapphire-blue depths. She bit her lip. 'I drove into Bridgeport yesterday... no, of course it wasn't yesterday, I'm all mixed up, it was the day before. I wanted to apologise to you——'

'Apologise? For what?'

Briony swallowed. 'For having called you a liar. Jake, I found out it was Polly who took the sign——'

'I know. She happened to mention what she'd done. I can see why you automatically blamed me. Apology accepted.' The impatience in Jake's tone left Briony in no doubt that as far as he was concerned the incident was forgotten. 'Now for God's sake will you get on with whatever it was you were going to say? You came to town to see me... and then what?'

Briony, grateful that the matter of the sign had been cleared up, directed her mind back to the previous slant of their conversation. 'Your secretary said you'd gone to the Pelican for lunch, so I went there, and...' She hesitated for a moment as she saw his brows lower in a dark frown, but before he could speak she rushed on, 'And I saw you with Angelique. It threw me; I didn't know you knew her, and I stepped behind a pillar to catch my breath... and as you passed——' her voice was low '—I heard the two of you talking.'

Jake's frown deepened. 'You'll have to refresh my memory,' he said steadily. 'What were Miss St Clair and I talking about at that point?'

Miss St Clair? The formality of his speech hit Briony like a slap. It was surely proof of his anger with her, his resentment at her eavesdropping. She took in a deep breath. Might as well get it over with. 'I heard enough to let me know exactly what was going on.'

His look was one of disbelief. 'And yet you still went to London? You were still prepared to go with Sharp? Dammit, you were in such a hurry to meet him, you didn't even wait to say goodbye?' His eyes were pools of utter bewilderment. 'It doesn't make sense——'

'Nothing makes much sense where strong emotions are involved.' Briony felt her cheeks turn pink. This was going to be the hard part. 'Jake, I've made a decision. It's not an easy one for me, but I know it's going to be the only one I can make. I have a wonderful contract to illustrate a series of books for Dorothy Marsden——'

'Yes,' he interrupted tersely. 'Polly told me.'

'So I can support myself and I want to move out. From the Crag. Permanently. It would be...awkward——' her lips moved in a bitter smile '—that's putting it mildly, isn't it?—for me to stay, now that...'

Briony looked away from him, unable to face him as she spoke the words that would drive him away forever. 'Now that I'm in love with you.' Her voice was husky with pain. 'I heard Angelique say yes, Jake, heard her agree to marry you. With her living here as your bride, it would be impossible for me to stay on at the Crag. I couldn't bear it...'

No, she couldn't bear it, and she couldn't bear being with Jake at such close quarters any longer. Letting her knife and fork drop with a clatter against the heavy china plate, she stumbled to her feet, and, without looking at him, she wheeled away and ran down the steps, through the main cabin, and into the small one where she'd slept earlier. Tears blinding her, she flung herself on to the narrow bunk, where she lay flat on her stomach, her face in the pillow, her arms circling her head. If only she could die. That's all she wanted to do. Die. Nothing but death could obliterate this agonising pain ripping at her heart. Nothing but death could heal her bleeding wounds.

She clenched her small hands into fists. Oh, Jake, she cried out silently, why couldn't things have been different? Why did I have to fall in love with you?

* * *

'Aren't you hungry, dear?' Polly frowned at Briony's dessert plate, the apple pie scarcely touched, and then looked anxiously at her across the walnut dining-table. 'You're usually starving after being out on the boat all day. You're not coming down with something, are you?'

I'm already down with something, Briony thought miserably. Unrequited love—there's an ailment guaranteed to put anyone off her food! 'I'm fine, Poll.' She hoped her smile was convincing but it felt weak and artificial.

'I'll have a second helping, thanks, Polly.' Jake passed over his plate, a grin lighting his handsome face.

Briony tore her eyes from him, and, twining her fingers together on her lap, kept her gaze fixed on them. How could he? He must know her heart was breaking, yet he was acting as if he didn't care. In fact, his mood over dinner had been lighter than she'd seen it in weeks. Was it because he'd been worrying about her reaction to learning he was going to be married? Had he and Angelique perhaps been afraid that she'd want to stay on at the Crag?

They hadn't talked after her confession in the yacht's cockpit. She had stayed below all afternoon, and he hadn't once come near her, and when he was busy tying up the boat on their return she'd slipped up to the house. She'd talked briefly with Polly, and then gone to the studio and started tidying up her things. And she hadn't seen Jake till Polly had rung the gong to announce that dinner was served and she'd bumped into him at the front door as he came back from somewhere in the Jag. Probably he'd been to see Angelique.

And all through dinner he'd treated her as he'd always treated her in the past, before this dreadful summer. Teasing, absent, affectionate. It was, of course, a front— a front he probably intended to keep up for Polly's sake, and one which he would be able to drop as soon as she, Briony, left the Crag for good as she'd promised.

With a sigh, she untwined her fingers. She just couldn't stand being in the same room as Jake, feeling his male impact even though she wasn't looking at him. Pushing back her chair, she stood up. 'Polly, if you'll excuse me, I'll go through and start the dishes——'

'Sit down, Briony.'

Startled by Jake's authoritative tone, Briony hesitated. Looking at him wide-eyed, she saw by the determined expression on his face that she had better obey him. Lips tight, she sank down into her chair again.

'What is it?' Her voice was thready.

Jake swallowed the last mouthful of his apple pie and arranged his spoon neatly on the blue and white plate. Pushing back his chair, he tilted it on its back legs and cupped his hands behind his head. Every aspect of his bearing was relaxed. 'I wanted to catch you both together,' he said lazily, 'because I have an announcement to make.'

He paused, his dark eyebrows raised as he waited for a response.

He didn't get one from Briony, but he did get one from his aunt.

'An announcement, Jake?' Polly's eyes gleamed with anticipation. 'About what, dear?'

Jake raked back his dark hair in a familiar gesture that made Briony's throat muscles constrict painfully. 'I'm going to get married.'

She thought the shock would stop her heart. Oh, not shock that he was getting married... that she already knew. But shock that he could be so cruel as to subject her to this, subject her to having to act out a pretence of delight in front of Polly. A chill seemed to take hold of her body, a chill that started her shivering. Vaguely, she heard Polly's exclamation of pleasure, heard her say, 'It's Diane, of course... how nice——'

'No, Poll. You're wrong. It's not Diane. Oh, we've always been very close, but that special something that should exist between two people in love didn't ever exist between us. We're good friends, and always will be...but that's all——'

'Then who, dear?' Polly made no secret of her puzzlement. 'I can't think who else it could be...'

'Congratulations, Jake.' Briony stared levelly at him. She had to admit that she felt a certain contempt for him, a contempt that was quite unfamiliar. She would never have guessed that he had such a cruel—or was it merely insensitive?—streak in him. 'And your bride——?'

'Oh, Jake, don't keep us in suspense any longer!' Polly's voice was pleading. 'Do tell us who she is—the new mistress of Devil's Crag.'

Jake chuckled. 'The new mistress of Devil's Crag. That's quite a title, isn't it? Rather impressive. But I'm sorry, I can't tell you who she is——'

'But why ever not?' Polly's cheeks were flushed.

'Because I haven't yet given the lady an engagement ring...'

'Oh, Jake,' Polly wailed, 'do you have to be so formal?'

With a fluid movement, Jake swung his chair forward and got to his feet. 'The woman I love is romantic,' he said softly. 'I don't think she'd appreciate my telling the world we're getting married until she has my ring on her finger.'

'When, Jake?' Briony forced herself to speak, just to keep Polly from noticing her anguished silence. 'Soon?'

'Tonight.'

'You're giving her the ring tonight?' Polly took in a deep breath. 'Oh, how thrilling!'

'And now——' Jake slanted a disarming smile at his aunt as he rounded the table to where Briony was sitting '—I'm going to steal Briony for a while, if you don't mind. Miss Campbell——' he bowed elegantly '—will you join me for a last walk together on the moors?'

Only her stubborn pride allowed Briony to conceal her revulsion from the cruelty of his invitation. Only her stubborn pride allowed her to give him a cool smile. 'I'll be delighted, Mr Trelawney. Just give me a moment to go upstairs and change out of these sandals.'

How she managed to walk across the room without breaking down, she would never know, but manage it she did. Upstairs in her bedroom, however, she collapsed on the bed and let the tears flow. When they ceased, she sponged her swollen eyes with a damp cloth, and as she stared at her stark reflection in the mirror she felt her heart harden.

She had been mistaken about Jake. There was a callous side to him that had never revealed itself to her before. She must keep remembering it. It would surely make her pain a little less unbearable, and make this last walk easier to endure.

'Give me your hand, Briony.'

Before she could draw it away, Jake had grasped her hand with his warm, lean fingers, and enclosed it in his. The sensation skimming up her arm was exquisite—like the exquisite agony in her heart, the dreadful ache closing her throat. Why couldn't it have been an ugly, raw day? Why was it one of those perfect August evenings when the Cornish moorland seemed like a corner of paradise? Scents of wild flowers, sounds of ocean and rustling breeze, air so clear and tangy that it was nectar in the lungs. Birds sang above, the heather rustled underfoot. And her hand was in the hand of the man she loved.

Only one thing was wrong. He didn't love her in return.

'I want to tell you about my relationship with Angelique,' he said, and she felt his fingers tighten their grip. 'Then you'll understand——'

'All right, Jake.' Briony concentrated on keeping her voice steady. 'I'm listening.'

'I haven't known her very long...we met, actually, in mid-June...'

A whirlwind romance. Briony tried to ignore the pain cutting through her. 'Where did you meet?' she managed.

'She came to my office——'

'Your office?' Despite her distress, Briony found herself repeating what he'd said, questioningly.

'Mm. She wanted to ask my advice.'

Briony looked up at Jake. He was frowning, his eyes fixed on the moor ahead. 'But surely,' she murmured, 'you can't talk about that? You're a lawyer...ethics forbid you to——'

His lips compressed. 'Oh, I know damned well about legal ethics, Briony. And that's where this whole problem lay...'

'I don't understand.'

'No, of course you don't.' He uttered a frustrated sigh. 'You don't know Angelique very well, do you?'

Briony shrugged. 'I know she's very...shy. Someone told me she'd been brought up by a very old-fashioned grandmother, and it's almost as if she's living in a different century.'

'That's all true.' Impatiently, Jake flicked away a small insect that was buzzing around his head. 'And that's why it was so difficult for her to talk to me. Difficult for me to help her. I had to coax the whole thing out of her...and she only told me after I'd given her my word that I'd not repeat her confidences to anyone, not even my partner, till she decided if she was going to press charges or not. She just couldn't make up her mind what to do...'

'Press charges? Against——?' Briony broke off. 'Oh, I'm sorry, Jake, I shouldn't even be asking you; you can't talk about——'

'I can talk. Angelique wants me to talk with you. In fact, she insisted I was to tell you everything before you went to London. You see, Bri, it was against Professor Sharp that she was considering pressing charges.'

Briony halted, and, sweeping her hand from his, stared up at him bewilderedly. 'Angelique...was going to...

Why?' But even as she formed the question in her mind the answer began to seep into her brain slowly, but inexorably. And as it did she found herself speaking her thoughts aloud. 'Angelique was the one he had originally asked to go on the tour... he told me she had backed out because she didn't have enough money. He told me he'd been disappointed in her work... and I thought he must have been, because I remember seeing her final marks posted, and though she passed her marks were borderline. I was shocked, because she'd always been a top student...'

'You have some of the facts, but not all, Bri.' Jake's expression was grim. 'He did ask her to go on the tour, and she did accept his invitation to travel with him and his wife. But what neither you nor anyone else knew was that when she went to his house to discuss the trip he... made a pass at her——'

The sound of Briony's little gasp interrupted his words for a moment, and then he went on, 'Rather an aggressive and unpleasant pass... not to mince words, he tried to force himself on her. Because of her inherent timidity, Angelique had difficulty fighting him off, but when she finally regained control of the situation he warned her that if she didn't co-operate he would drastically reduce her marks.'

'She didn't, obviously, co-operate. And after agonising over the situation she came to you for legal advice?' Briony surmised.

'That's right.' The breeze blew Jake's black hair over his eyes, and he brushed it back abruptly. 'Though lord knows how she ever found the courage. Then you came home and told me you were going abroad with that *bastard*——'

'Oh, Jake.' In a blinding flash everything fell into place in Briony's mind. 'You couldn't tell me. How awful for you.'

'Awful?' Jake gave a mirthless laugh. 'It was sheer hell to have to stand back helplessly and watch you walk into a situation that could have had consequences that didn't bear thinking about. That *I* couldn't bear to think about!'

'But...you say Angelique finally freed you to tell me? How did that happen?'

'The day you saw us at the Pelican—we'd had an appointment in my office earlier, and Angelique had told me she had to make a decision one way or the other, because she couldn't stand the strain any longer. She started to cry, and I suggested we talk about it over lunch. I took her through to my private rooms first so she could tidy up... and she happened to notice our photo on the mantelpiece. That's when I found out she'd heard via Price that you were going abroad with Sharp; she asked me how I knew you... and I told her.' He shrugged. 'You can guess the rest...'

'She insisted I be told about the professor, despite her desire to keep her own experience secret. Oh, Jake...what has she decided to do? Is she going to press charges?'

Jake nodded. 'We've already presented an appeal to the college board to have her final marks reviewed, and yes,' he went on grimly, 'she's going to charge him with attempted rape. Of course, it will just be her word alone, against his, and she feels that with his influence she won't stand a chance. But she's determined to go ahead. And even if the bastard does go free, then at least she'll feel she's done all she can to——'

'You'll get a conviction, Jake. You always do. Besides, it won't be her word alone.' Briony's voice trembled but it was clear. 'I'll back her up.'

She felt a chill run down her spine as she saw Jake's expression change, saw his face take on a grey cast. He gripped her arms. 'For God's sake, Bri, he didn't——?'

'He...didn't...not what you're thinking, Jake. But that evening, when I was at his home, he did make a pass at me.' Her laugh was mirthless. 'I was so naïve—

I thought I was mistaken! But that little incident, coupled with the things he said to me at the airport, the... the horrid way he treated me there, right out in the open...' She shuddered. 'Oh, Jake, when I saw you at the airport, I'd already told him I wasn't going with him. He's... despicable.'

'Oh, my God... So when I dragged you away——'

'You weren't dragging me, Jake. I came willingly.'

He didn't say anything for a long moment, and then, in a voice that was soft but intense, he asked, 'Are you sure you want to go ahead with this, Bri? Do you know what you're getting into?'

'Yes, I'm sure...and no, I don't know what I'm getting into—it's not something I've done before. But if we don't stop him he might assault someone else.'

'You're quite a girl, Bri——'

'Not a girl!' Briony shook her head fiercely and her blonde hair swung in a shimmering curtain around her cheeks. She swept it back with her hands. 'I'm a woman, Jake. And now that we're bringing everything out into the open I think it's time I let you know just how furious you've made me by not admitting—or even noticing!— that fact. I'm a woman!' She glared at him, her grey eyes sparking like diamonds. 'A woman... *dammit*!' Her frustrated cry rang out across the heather.

To her astonishment, Jake smiled. Such a smile it was, too—lighting up his face as if the sun were shining right on it... yet his back was to the sun! His blue eyes were warm, and she had never seen him look so... so *happy*! He was laughing at her. She could tell. And as she stared up at him, her mind stumbling around in confusion, he reached out and pulled her into his arms. Too stunned to resist, she just slumped there against his warm chest, feeling the strong, steady drumbeats of his heart against her shoulder, hardly noticing the sharp edge of something in his shirt pocket as it dug into her flesh.

'Oh, I know you're a woman, Briony.' His voice was husky, enveloping her like a comforting blanket. 'I've known that for some time...since, I think, your surprise party, though I tried to deny it to myself.'

Briony closed her eyes as she felt his lips brush tenderly across her brow. Bliss. The warmth of the sun, the scent of the moor and the ocean...this man who was holding her, and the male scent of his skin and hair...it all added up to bliss.

Except for one thing. He wasn't her man. He belonged to someone else.

She tried to pull away, but he kept her in the sturdy circle of his arms. 'Angelique,' she said weakly, 'you're going to see her tonight? Give her...the ring?'

'Ah, the ring.' He drew back a little and took something from his shirt pocket. She saw that the thing that had been jutting into her shoulder was a dusky pink velvet-covered box. 'You'd like to see it.'

Of course she didn't want to see it. But before she could protest he'd opened the lid. Briony felt as if her throat were closing up with emotion as she looked at the perfect oriental amethyst, set in platinum. 'It's beautiful,' she breathed. 'The most beautiful ring I've ever seen.'

'Try it on,' he offered silkily. 'I'd like to see how it looks.'

'Oh, no! What on earth would Angelique think if she knew——?'

'Angelique need never know.' In a movement so swift, so smooth, that it was completed before she had time to realise what was happening, he slipped the ring on to her finger.

'There,' he said, a smug sound in his voice, 'a perfect fit, and looks absolutely wonderful on your adorable, artistic hand. What do you think?' He looped his arms around her and grinned down into her astonished face.

Briony stared up at him. 'Have you gone completely mad?' she demanded. 'You buy a ring for one woman, and you place it on the hand of another——'

'Uh-uh,' he responded firmly. 'One and the same woman.'

She was the one who had gone completely mad, she decided. She couldn't make sense of a word he was saying. What did he mean, 'One and the same woman'?

'One and the same woman,' he repeated, his chuckle having a distinctly mischievous ring to it. 'My woman. The woman I love.'

Briony felt as if her legs were buckling under her. Weakly she clutched Jake's shirt. 'But Angelique,' she whispered. 'I heard you clearly... heard you tell her you were so glad she had finally decided to say, "Yes!"'

Jake pulled her hard up against him. 'If you had been listening earlier, my darling eavesdropper, you'd have known she was saying, yes, she'd press charges against Sharp...'

'Not saying yes to you? You didn't propose to her?'

'Of course I didn't propose to her, you sweet little idiot! Our relationship is strictly professional. And, though Angelique is pretty enough in her own quiet way, by no stretch of the imagination would I call her beautiful. And didn't I tell you once that the woman I loved was *very* beautiful?'

Beautiful? Jake was talking about her? He thought she was *beautiful*? Briony looked up at his lean, tanned features and saw them through a distinctly rosy glow... a glow which undoubtedly came from the rainbow in the sky. Though why she should be seeing a rainbow, when there hadn't been any rain, she really didn't know! 'You mean... *I'm* the one you're going to marry?'

'Oh, my love, yes, yes, yes.' Jake's lips were sweet as the first day of summer as they claimed hers in a kiss that set her heart skipping about like an intoxicated lamb. A kiss that set her senses into a mindless, ecstatic orbit. When finally he paused for a moment so that she could catch her breath, he murmured in her hair, 'Yes, you're the one I'm going to marry. You're mine. Forever. Just as I'm yours.'

'But Jake, at dinner you said you wanted to take me for one last walk on the moors——'

'If you'll cast your mind back,' he said in a gently mocking voice, 'I invited a certain *Miss Campbell* for one last walk on the moors. I intend walking there many, many times with...Mrs Jacob Trelawney...'

Briony wondered if it was possible to die of utter ecstasy. 'But why...why didn't you tell me you loved me—today, on the yacht, when I confessed how I felt about you?'

'That,' he groaned, 'was the most difficult thing I have ever had to do in my life: to stay on deck, knowing you loved me, knowing you were curled up below on your bunk, so soft and vulnerable. I knew that if I went down to comfort you I wouldn't have been able to stop myself from making love to you.'

'You...said the woman you loved was...innocent.' Briony blushed. 'I am, Jake.'

'You don't have to tell me that, Bri,' he said gently. 'I know. Your eyes have that special shine.'

'I think, all along, without realising it, I was waiting...for you.'

'And I think, all along, I was waiting for you to grow up, though I didn't realise it either.' He held her so tightly that she could scarcely breathe. 'Ever since you came home you've been driving me to distraction—and I couldn't figure out why! When we were together, I couldn't be civil to you, but when we were apart I found myself thinking of you constantly. It wasn't till the night of the dance, and I held you in my arms in the rose garden, that I understood the reason for my confusion. I'd fallen in love with you.'

'Oh, Jake...that was the night I knew I was in love with you! Why did you fight your feelings?'

'Bri, when your ma died, I promised myself I'd protect you—from men who would try to take advantage of you. So when I began wanting you myself I felt as if I wasn't much better than that bastard Sharp! Every time we touched, I wanted to pull you into my arms... but when you did end up there I forced myself to push you away because I wasn't sure if I could control myself. Only when I knew that what I felt was more—so much more!—than desire, that I had actually fallen head over heels in love with you——'

'Oh, Jake, won't Polly be thrilled? And she can stay on with us, can't she?'

But she knew Jake's answer before he gave it. After kissing her again thoroughly, he said in a husky voice, 'I want you to have the wedding-day you deserve, my love. You'll be the most beautiful bride that ever was, in a white lace dress——'

'From the Jasmine Boutique?' Briony teased.

He twined a lock of her long hair around one index finger and gave it a gentle tug. 'Where else, my little jungle cat?' He ran his lips across the shining blonde strands. 'As long as I live I'll never forget looking in through the glass door and seeing you in that exotic leopard-skin outfit. You roused such primitive feelings in me——'

'So that's why you were so upset... not because I was late.' Briony's voice was a seductive purr. 'And when you were so rude to my dear friend Tony at the theatre——'

'I wanted to punch that young Tarzan look-alike on the jaw when I saw him swing you up in his arms!'

'So that's why you were reading the programme upside-down a few minutes later,' Briony said demurely.

'I was?' Jake glowered at her. 'You minx——'

'And when you found me on the beach wearing just my bikini bottom, and you stared at my naked breasts——'

'Briony——' There was a note of grim warning in Jake's voice. 'Don't do this to me... not if you want to wear white on your wedding-day...'

Briony twined her arms round his neck and pressed her lips against his throat before looking up at him, her eyes bright with laughter...and something else. 'Pure white never did suit me very well, Jake! Perhaps...on my wedding-day...an off-white might be more attractive? Or even black...I believe it's quite a fashionable colour for the bride these days.'

As she heard Jake give a defeated groan she felt sheer happiness exploding inside her. At last the man she loved knew she was a woman, at last he accepted it. Accepted what she was going to be...and wanted to be...for the rest of her life.

His woman.

Trelawney's Woman.

Next Month's Romances

Each month you can choose from a wide variety of romance with Mills & Boon. Below are the new titles to look out for next month, why not ask either Mills & Boon Reader Service or your Newsagent to reserve you a copy of the titles you want to buy — just tick the titles you would like and either post to Reader Service or take it to any Newsagent and ask them to order your books.

Please save me the following titles:	Please tick	√
BACHELOR AT HEART	Roberta Leigh	
TIDEWATER SEDUCTION	Anne Mather	
SECRET ADMIRER	Susan Napier	
THE QUIET PROFESSOR	Betty Neels	
ONE-NIGHT STAND	Sandra Field	
THE BRUGES ENGAGEMENT	Madeleine Ker	
AND THEN CAME MORNING	Daphne Clair	
AFTER ALL THIS TIME	Vanessa Grant	
CONFRONTATION	Sarah Holland	
DANGEROUS INHERITANCE	Stephanie Howard	
A MAN FOR CHRISTMAS	Annabel Murray	
DESTINED TO LOVE	Jennifer Taylor	
AN IMAGE OF YOU	Liz Fielding	
TIDES OF PASSION	Sally Heywood	
DEVIL'S DREAM	Nicola West	
HERE COMES TROUBLE	Debbie Macomber	

If you would like to order these books in addition to your regular subscription from Mills & Boon Reader Service please send £1.70 per title to: Mills & Boon Reader Service, P.O. Box 236, Croydon, Surrey, CR9 3RU; quote your Subscriber No:..
(If applicable) and complete the name and address details below. Alternatively, these books are available from many local Newsagents including W.H.Smith, J.Menzies, Martins and other paperback stockists from 4th December 1992.

Name:..
Address:..
....Post Code:............................
To Retailer: If you would like to stock M&B books please contact your regular book/magazine wholesaler for details.

You may be mailed with offers from other reputable companies as a result of this application.
If you would rather not take advantage of these opportunities please tick box ☐

Mills & Boon

Four brand new romances from favourite Mills & Boon authors have been specially selected to make your Christmas special.

THE FINAL SURRENDER
Elizabeth Oldfield

SOMETHING IN RETURN
Karen van der Zee

HABIT OF COMMAND
Sophie Weston

CHARADE OF THE HEART
Cathy Williams

Published in November 1992   Price: £6.80

Available from Boots, Martins, John Menzies, W.H. Smith, most supermarkets and other paperback stockists. Also available from Mills & Boon Reader Service, PO Box 236, Thornton Road, Croydon, Surrey CR9 3RU.

BARBARY WHARF

Will Gina Tyrrell succeed in her plans to oust
Nick Caspian from the Sentinel –
or will Nick fight back?

There is only one way for Nick to win, but it might,
in the end, cost him everything!

The final book in the Barbary Wharf series

SURRENDER

Available from November 1992   Price: £2.99

W●RLDWIDE

*Available from Boots, Martins, John Menzies, W.H. Smith,
most supermarkets and other paperback stockists.
Also available from Mills & Boon Reader Service, PO Box 236,
Thornton Road, Croydon, Surrey CR9 3RU.*

4 FREE

Romances and 2 FREE gifts just for you!

You can enjoy all the heartwarming emotion of true love for FREE! Discover the heartbreak and the happiness, the emotion and the tenderness of the modern relationships in Mills & Boon Romances.

We'll send you 4 captivating Romances as a special offer from Mills & Boon Reader Service, along with the chance to have 6 Romances delivered to your door each month.

Claim your FREE books and gifts overleaf...

An irresistible offer from Mills & Boon

Here's a personal invitation from Mills & Boon Reader Service, to become a regular reader of Romances. To welcome you, we'd like you to have 4 books, a CUDDLY TEDDY and a special MYSTERY GIFT absolutely FREE.

Then you could look forward each month to receiving 6 brand new Romances, delivered to your door, postage and packing free! Plus our free Newsletter featuring author news, competitions, special offers and much more.

This invitation comes with no strings attached. You may cancel or suspend your subscription at any time, and still keep your free books and gifts.

It's so easy. Send no money now. Simply fill in the coupon below and post it to -
**Reader Service, FREEPOST,
PO Box 236, Croydon, Surrey CR9 9EL.**

NO STAMP REQUIRED

Free Books Coupon

Yes! Please rush me 4 free Romances and 2 free gifts! Please also reserve me a Reader Service subscription. If I decide to subscribe I can look forward to receiving 6 brand new Romances each month for just £10.20, postage and packing free. If I choose not to subscribe I shall write to you within 10 days - I can keep the books and gifts whatever I decide. I may cancel or suspend my subscription at any time. I am over 18 years of age.

Ms/Mrs/Miss/Mr_____ EP31R

Address _____

_____

Postcode_____ Signature _____

Offer expires 31st May 1993. The right is reserved to refuse an application and change the terms of this offer. Readers overseas and in Eire please send for details. Southern Africa write to Book Services International Ltd, P.O. Box 42654, Craighall, Transvaal 2024. You may be mailed with offers from other reputable companies as a result of this application.

If you would prefer not to share in this opportunity, please tick box ☐